Brawl in Bardo

In This Series

DAGMARMIURA.COM

Brawl in Bardo

Brawl in Bardo

George Bixley

DAGMAR MIURA

LOS ANGELES

Published by Dagmar Miura
Los Angeles
www.dagmarmiura.com

Brawl in Bardo

Copyright © 2019, 2023 Dagmar Miura
All rights reserved. No part of this book may be used or reproduced
in any manner whatsoever without prior written permission except
in the case of brief quotations embodied in critical articles or
reviews. For information, address Dagmar Miura, dagmarmiura@
gmail.com, or visit our website at www.dagmarmiura.com.

This is a work of fiction. Names, characters, businesses, places,
events, and incidents are either the products of the author's imag-
ination or used in a fictitious manner. Any resemblance to actual
persons, living or dead, or actual events is purely coincidental.

First published 2019

ISBN: 978-1-951130-01-5

ONE

S later swung the baseball bat, connecting with the flowerpot Max had tossed for him. It struck with a satisfying *crack,* and the pot disintegrated into a million pieces. They came down here to do this sometimes, he and Max, to the recycling warehouse that belonged to one of Max's clients. The guy had picked up a truckload of counterfeit terra-cotta pots, made of sand and dirt and pink dye, useless for anything besides blowing off steam. The pallets sat behind the building in a small yard, littered with pink rubble and lit tonight by the glaring outdoor lights high above. The client had worked his way through half a pallet after Max confirmed his wife's infidelity, and part of his payment was giving them access to the yard.

"My turn," Max said, waggling his fingers for the bat. Slater handed it over and went to the pallets to collect a stack of little pots, then tossed one in a gentle arc. Max swung at it and connected with a resounding *crack*, turning it into a cloud of pink dust.

"I wanted to ask for your help," Max said, raising the bat above his shoulder again. "It's kind of about Vanessa." He nodded for another pot.

Slater tossed one, congratulating him with a guttural "Yeah" when he vaporized it. He thought something might be up, as Max had been quieter than usual. No surprise that it was girlfriend trouble—Vanessa was in a completely different social stratum, working as an academic at a good school, and Max was basically a thug—a PI with his gut hanging over his belt, his sidearm bulging under his jacket. At least tonight he'd left his weapon in the office, and had taken off his suit jacket to swing the bat. The elastic strap on the safety goggles he was wearing to keep the detritus out of his eyes made his mousy hair stick out in misshapen tufts. But they had a rapport, he and Max, and they had set up shop together in a little office in the Fashion District. Mostly they each worked alone and split the rent, but Max actually had a PI license, which gave Slater access to a lot more tools for his own jobs.

"What's up with Vanessa?" Slater said, and tossed another pot.

Max struck it a glancing blow, slamming it down onto the gritty asphalt.

"I need to track down her brother. His name is Jordan. He jumped bail in Vegas. That kid owes me fourteen grand."

"Ouch," Slater said, glad that he hadn't said what had first come to mind: *Did she finally dump you?* "What was he charged with?"

"Robbery." Max set the tip of the bat on the ground. "I'm going after him."

"Robbery or armed robbery? What kind of person are you dealing with?"

"He went into a medical office and pulled a gun on the doctor."

"So the cops will assume he's armed."

"Exactly. They're looking for a black guy with a gun. You know what that means."

"He's going to get ventilated."

"That's why I want to haul him in myself. At least he'll stay alive."

Slater waved for the bat and exchanged it for the stack of flowerpots, then stepped over to where Max had been standing and readied the bat.

"Where did he get the weapon?"

"Jordan wouldn't tell me." He tossed a pot and waited for Slater to swing and pulverize it. "I'm not even sure where to start looking. He ditched his cell phone, and he left his car parked at Vanessa's place."

"Even if he gets another phone, he'll use his accounts," Slater said, and nodded for another pitch.

"Vanessa's watching for him online. There's been nothing since he missed his arraignment." Max ducked as Slater's swing sent a big pink shard tumbling toward his head. "Nice."

"There are other ways to track people down. We can work on it back at the office," Slater said, and readied the bat.

Max tossed a pot. "I'm glad I asked."

After a few more swings, Slater handed Max the bat and pitched again for him. Despite the cool evening, he was sweating, and wiped his brow with the back of his hand. It was that humid overcast season that hit Los Angeles after the spring, with the gray days that made people placid for a while before the summer heat brought out all the aggression.

Once he'd turned several little pots into dusty pink debris, Max offered him the bat.

"I'm ready to go," Slater said, and took the bat, leaning it against one of the pallets of pots.

Before they went in, he dusted off his jeans and his shirt, then pulled off his goggles and ruffled his black hair with his fingers, dislodging as much of the pink grit as he could.

Stepping inside, they walked across the warehouse floor toward the loading docks. The place was surprisingly clean, considering they processed garbage. Bales of colorful plastic were stacked up in neat squares with wide aisles between them. Rather than the stench of decaying organic matter, the place smelled like machine oil and electric motors.

Max hung the goggles they'd borrowed on the wall rack in the locker room. As they walked toward the loading docks, a worker in a blue uniform approached them. Eyeing Slater, she said something in Spanish. It happened all the time in this city—Slater had his father's dark Latin coloring, and looked like he should speak the language.

"*No entiendo,*" Slater said.

Not missing a beat, she asked, "Was the boss out there playing baseball with you guys?"

"You mean Andrés?" Max said. "I haven't seen him tonight."

She acknowledged that and walked toward the back of the warehouse.

"Andrés doesn't mind you coming in to smash stuff when he's not around?" Slater said.

Max waved a hand at the vast space. "It's not like there's anything to steal. It's all trash."

One of the loading docks was unoccupied, with the big door rolled open, and they hopped down and walked across the yard, past the row of big roll-off dumpsters parked there, and out to the street through the pedestrian gate. Other times they'd parked inside, but the vehicle gate had been closed when they got here.

Parked at the curb just past the driveway was Slater's classic Thunderbird, its black paint gleaming under the street lights. The industrial neighborhood was mostly deserted this late in the evening, and he'd hesitated to leave it out here. Standing next to the Thunderbird's driver's door was a tall guy, bent over, peering inside.

"Damn it," Slater muttered, and quickened his pace.

The guy didn't notice them at first, and as Slater got closer, he saw why—he had earbuds jammed into his ears. When Slater stepped into the street behind the car, he finally looked up, surprise on his face.

"What's up?" he said, pulling his earphones out and taking a step back.

Slater came up to him and grabbed his shirt collar, evoking a surprised yelp. That look on his face—they always had that look, a mix of anger and fear. The guy was tall, but he was lanky, and easy to manipulate.

"Hey," he shouted, pawing at Slater's face. "Let me go."

Slater swatted his hands away and hustled

him backward onto the sidewalk, then shoved him against the metal fence of the recycling yard. Max stood nearby, watchful, ready to step in if need be. The guy tried to throw a punch, but Slater blocked it and hooked his boot behind his calf, shoving him off balance. As he twisted to the side, Slater reached around and groped in the small of his back, then pulled out the tool that he knew was hidden there, tucked into his belt—a flat piece of sprung steel with notches cut into the edge, used by thieves and cops alike to break into cars. Grabbing his collar again, Slater slapped his face, left and then right, a rapid kovac.

"What the hell?" the guy shouted, stumbling away. "I was just looking at your rig."

"Is that why you're packing a slim jim?" Slater said, waving it in his face.

He trotted a few paces down the sidewalk before he paused to look at Max, then at Slater. "Can I have that back?"

"You're lucky I don't flatten you," Slater said. "Keep moving."

He went a few more paces and turned to shout, "Freaking *cholo*."

"Don't make me come after you," Slater called to him.

Once the guy was farther up the block, Slater went to the back of the Thunderbird and opened the trunk, tossing the tool inside.

"Hang on to it," Max said. "Those can be handy."

"It looks like a cheap one," Slater said, and slammed the trunk.

"No surprise. That guy was skinny like a junkie."

"He also had meth mouth," Slater said, walking around to the driver's side. "At least we caught him before he messed up my door."

"One less involuntary contribution to the drug trade," Max said as he climbed in.

After he started the throaty engine, Slater slipped it into gear and pulled away from the curb, navigating north under the 10 freeway, back toward their office. Los Angeles was still a manufacturing center for the clothing industry, and their neighborhood was a hodgepodge of fabric suppliers, manufacturers, and even retail storefronts, all dead quiet at this hour.

Slater pulled into the nearly empty surface lot across the street from their building, and before he got out, grabbed a paper bag from the backseat. Max shrugged on his suit jacket, and they strolled across and into the lobby.

A century ago, when it was new, this had been an office building, but today most of the tenants were sewing factories. Rent was a lot cheaper than in the new part of downtown, and setting up shop here, out of the way, almost obscured among the garment trade, meant they could operate with a lower profile.

"What's in the bag?" Max said, eyeing it as they boarded the elevator.

"I'll show you when we get upstairs."

The doors rumbled shut and they lurched upward. On the ninth floor they exited and walked around behind the shaft to the door with their names on it:

SLATER IBÁÑEZ

MAXIMILLIAN CONROY

INVESTIGATIONS

The front office had a coatrack and a desk that nobody used, and off the sides was an office for each of them. Max's had the window, with a view of the brick wall next door, and behind Slater's desk sat their old-school safe, bolted to the concrete floor.

Slater flicked on the lights and opened the paper bag, revealing a little plaster statue of a skeleton. It was wearing a crown, and one hand rested on a scythe, its blade idle. He set it on the desk.

"That's pretty grim," Max said, picking it up to examine it. "Is it for Day of the Dead?"

"Different kind of skeleton. He's called Rey Pascual. How do you feel about him hanging out in the front office?"

Max set it down and furrowed his brow. "Is he that narco saint?"

"They're related, maybe, but this is the male version. It was a gift from the woman I get *pupusas* from. She says it'll bring good business."

"Let me get used to him for a couple of days."

"It can go in my office if it doesn't fit here," Slater said. "I'm not a good judge of that stuff."

"So what was your idea about tracking down Jordan?"

"Bring a chair," Slater said, and went into his little office.

Max rolled his desk chair in and sat at the side of his desk.

"So you know how everything we do online is tracked by the cell companies and the internet providers and the app developers?"

Max nodded. "Sure."

"There are third-party businesses that aggregate and sell all that information. They're called data brokers."

"Can you use the data to get someone's physical location?"

"Not directly," Slater said, "but you can get awfully close. The brokers collate all the data about people into profiles, and we can buy those. They omit the specifics like your name and your driver's license number, but you can still identify people."

"Isn't it just stuff like where you go, and what you buy?"

"There's also a whole lot of speculative data that's generated from the real data. The software can look at what time of day you buy groceries, and what brand of cereal you eat, and predict whether you drink beer or wine or abstain altogether. It can compare the furniture you buy to the floor map of your house that your robot vacuum sent in, and then decide when you'll be in the market for new carpeting."

Max sighed. "It's very Big Brother."

"And we can use it. Even if the data doesn't include Jordan's current location, we can look at his profile to get some ideas."

"Can you pull a profile using someone's name?"

"No, but we can input all the details we have on the guy. Things that a data harvest would have picked up—his demographics, zip code, the car he drives. If we have enough detail, we might be able to narrow it down to his profile."

"Let's do it," Max said. "I know lots about him."

Slater wiggled the mouse on his desktop and pulled up a data broker, then clicked through to the form with the array of categories. Max rattled off Jordan's age, and where he'd lived, and what he knew about his education.

"What about music?" Slater said, peering at the screen.

"Wu Tang Clan, all day long."

After they'd entered as much information as Max could remember, Slater submitted it, then leaned back in his chair and rubbed his eyes.

"It's Friday night," Max said. "Will we get something by tomorrow, or will it have to wait for Monday?"

"It's all done by software. We should get results soon."

Max stifled a yawn. "Silly humans and their pesky office hours."

Sitting up again, Slater checked his email. "There it is." He turned the screen so Max could see the message, a list of different data sets and the prices for each.

"Christ, it's not cheap."

"So we have to pick the right set," Slater said, and scrolled down the list.

Max jabbed a finger at the screen. "That one only has nineteen people in it."

Slater read the summary: "nonsmoking, male, youth, minority, urban, View Park."

"That's definitely where he lives. Let's try it." He pulled out his wallet and handed Slater a credit card, and within a few minutes the full data set landed in his inbox.

"There's so much information," Slater said, clicking through the documents. "Each one of these profiles has dozens of pages."

"Can we print them out?" Max said.

Slater sent it all to the laser printer that sat against the wall at the end of his desk. It hummed to life and dutifully began spitting out pages. When it ran out of paper, Max went to get more from his desk, and before long they had several stacks of printouts. First they separated them into individual profiles, then started reading.

"I'm figuring out how to parse it," Max said, "but it's hard to tell what's hard data and what's just a guess."

"Here's something—regular trips to the waterfront at San Pedro. I bet this guy worked in shipping."

"Nobody ever said Jordan was connected to that industry."

"So this one's out," Slater said, and dropped the sheaf of pages on the floor.

"This guy's a gun owner," Max said. "He's out too."

"Even though Jordan used a weapon in the robbery?"

"Vanessa said he never had a gun before. Apparently he wasn't a hoodlum until now. That's the reason we bailed him out—the robbery was so out of character."

"Maybe she's deluded about her brother. He's all sweetness and light with her, and after dark he's a stone-cold gangbanger."

"It's possible. I don't know the kid that well. She has good judgment, but anybody can be fooled by a con artist."

They went back to weeding through the profiles, and eventually there were only three stacks of paper left. Max was hunched over Slater's desk, poring over a raft of pages, his eyes bleary.

"I can't see it," he said. "These three look like the same person. Any one of them could be Jordan."

"Is there a line in yours for junk food?" Slater said. "This guy makes 84 percent of his junk food purchases at burger places, and this one is 62 percent chicken."

Max flipped through the sheets. "This one is a true Angeleno—half tacos and half burgers."

"What kind of junk does Jordan eat?"

"Vanessa would know." He pulled out his phone and peered at it, tapping with a thick finger, then held it to his ear. "Sorry to wake you … So if Jordan was going for fast food, would he get tacos, or burgers, or chicken? … What if he had to pick one?" He listened for a moment longer, then said, "Thanks, sweet pea. Go back to sleep."

"What's the verdict?" Slater said.

"She said, 'Please don't eat trash.' Apparently Jordan would go for the tacos." He tapped one of the stacks of paper. "This might be our guy."

"Excellent. Next, we identify his phone."

"I'm assuming he ditched it and then got another one. I didn't see phone numbers in any of this stuff."

"Even better than the number is the phone's IMEI. It's like the serial number for the device, and it doesn't change even if you swap SIM cards. All of these profiles have a list of IMEIs associated with the person."

Max picked up the stack and flipped through the pages. "There's four of them listed for this guy. Who has four cell phones?"

"Most people, including you, if you count the ones you've thrown away. Each one should be dated. What's the most recent?"

"You're right—the oldest was first seen ten years ago. The last one is this week." Max looked up, his gaze intent. "It's actually the day he missed his arraignment. A new phone. This has to be him."

"My buddy Andy might have a way to get his current location from that IMEI number."

"I have a better idea," Max said, a smile spreading across his face. "I know a guy who works at one of the cell carriers. I've paid him before to find people for me. He's expensive because it's so damn shady, but he gets results in real time."

Max rose and went over to his office, taking the relevant sheet with him. His contact must have picked up the phone, as Slater heard him get into a conversation. Tuning it out, he started stacking the scattered paper that littered his desk and the floor, keeping the piles in order in case their assessment was wrong, in case they had to revisit all this. A minute later, Max came back.

"Got him," he said, his eyes bright.

"That was fast. Your contact was at work?"

"He said he was in bed already, but he can log in from anywhere. It's easier for him to find an IMEI than an actual phone number."

"So where is Jordan?" Slater demanded, leaning back in his chair.

"For the last three days, that new phone has been connected to the same cell tower in Barstow."

"That's not far away."

"Plus he's stationary, which makes him easier to find. This guy is going to send me a coverage map for the cell tower."

"It's not a big town," Slater said. "We'll find him."

"I'll ask Vanessa whether she knows about any Barstow connection."

"Don't do that. She might start her own investigating, and tip someone off."

Max nodded. "Good thinking."

Pushing himself up out of his chair, Slater stretched and arched his back. "We'll drive up there tomorrow?"

"You did it, brother," Max said, and held up his palm.

Slater met it in a satisfying slap. "That was the easy part. Thank me once we catch the fucker."

On the way out, before he flicked off the lights, Max looked at the skeleton statue on the front-office desk and said, "Good night, Rey."

In the elevator Slater pulled out his phone and texted Andy:

You awake?

His reply came a moment later:

Come over.

As they walked into the parking lot, Max pressed his key fob, eliciting a chirp from his matte-gray Challenger, parked next to Slater's car.

"Can we take your ride tomorrow?" Slater said. "I'm not sure the Thunderbird is up to it."

"The curse of the classic-car owner," Max said. "It'll have to be a bit later. I'm meeting a guy here in the morning about a window-shade job. At least I think it's a guy—the name is Leslie."

"That definitely could go either way."

"Just like the guys you date," he said, raising his eyebrows.

Slater chuckled at that. "Pick me up at my place after your meeting."

 TWO

Andy lived on Broadway, and Slater drove the few blocks through Skid Row into that part of downtown. The surface lot behind Andy's building was still crowded, reflecting the large number of bars and restaurants nearby, and he paid the attendant the flat evening rate, then walked around to the entrance.

The building had been a warehouse, more recently converted into lofts, with traces of its former incarnation still visible in the scuffed board floors and the big multipaned windows. Slater rapped on Andy's door and waited.

When he pulled it open, Andy was wearing a tank top and boxer shorts, and flashed him that perfect smile. His brown hair was a tousled mess, like it always was, and he was in need of a shave.

Slater followed him in, eyeing his tight little butt, and felt the familiar blast of air-conditioning. Andy kept the place chilly, as something about his CP made his metabolism run hot.

His loft was mostly one big room, with a bed in the corner and a desk with big computer screens. Slater eyed the little red electric scooter parked under the tattersall windows. He hated that thing, or maybe he hated the idea of that thing. Andy could walk, albeit not fast and with an uneven gait, but he did pretty well, especially when he used his sticks. Slater's thinking was, use it or lose it. But that didn't seem to translate to Andy's disability. He claimed he benefited from resting his muscles sometimes, and said the scooter was useful to get to the supermarket and the drugstore without waiting around for a car.

The TV set was on and muted—he really had been awake.

"You're sober," Andy said, stopping beside the little dining table and studying his face.

"I've been working."

"It's late. I guess that's the … nature of your job."

"Late nights and lowlifes," Slater said, and stepped closer, cradling Andy's head in his hands, running his fingers into his tangled hair, feeling the rhythmic random muscle movements in his neck.

"Your hair is all sweaty," Slater said, and leaned in, meeting the warmth of his taut mouth, exploring it.

Getting into it, Andy pulled him closer, his hands on Slater's back. As he pressed into him, Slater could feel that he was already hard.

He whispered in Slater's ear, "I'm going to … fuck you senseless."

"Bring it on," Slater growled, and followed him to the bed.

Mostly it was bluster; in reality things usually went a little more tamely. He let Andy push him backward onto the bed, and waited as he climbed up to straddle Slater, then grabbed his belt and started to undo the buckle. Slater knew better by now than to help him, and watched as he worked it loose, gradually making progress despite his lack of fine motor control. Slater slid his jeans off, and took off his shirt, and then pulled off Andy's. Andy squeezed his engorged cock, which made him gasp, and he leaned up to lock onto his mouth.

Andy dug for a condom in the bedside drawer, and Slater rolled it on for him, and slathered the lube, then shifted onto his side, guiding Andy with his hand. He groaned with the intensity of Andy pushing his way inside him. Starting slowly, eventually he was pounding him, and thrashing wildly, until he came. Slater turned to face him, mouthing his jaw and his neck, and grabbed the lube, squeezing it onto himself and then pulling Andy closer, thrusting between his thighs. With his arms wrapped around Andy's torso, his nose in his hair, breathing in his heady scent, he came, shuddering with the intensity of it. Afterward, Slater rolled onto his side and caught his breath.

"Can you grab a towel?" Andy said.

Slater got up and brought it from the bathroom, tossing it on the floor once he'd cleaned up. He shifted close to Andy, draping his arm across his belly. When he caught himself drifting into sleep, he sat up.

"I have to go."

"No, you don't," Andy said.

"I have a road trip tomorrow."

"There's booze here, and my bed is warmer than yours."

Slater ran his hands over Andy's warm skin for a while, massaging his muscles, then got up and went to the cupboard beside the refrigerator. Andy kept a handle of bourbon for him, and he unscrewed the cap, pouring it into a glass until it was half full. He hated having to limit his consumption like this, like a sailor on rations, but these were the new booze rules—a sobriety plan so that he wouldn't overdo it, wouldn't lose his memory of the evening and do stupid things, wouldn't have to start going to meetings.

He slammed the heady amber contents of the

glass, closing his eyes for a moment to relish the burn in his throat. After he flicked off the room lights, he climbed back into bed, wrapping an arm around Andy's torso, lulled to sleep by the rhythm of his heartbeat.

———•———

When he woke, daylight was streaming in the windows. Andy was sitting at his computer, absorbed in the screen, with his gauntlets on. The black sheaths fit onto his arms and functioned as computer input, somehow compensating for his imprecise muscle control and allowing him to work.

Andy must have felt him watching from the bed, and looked over.

"You're awake. What's on … your agenda today?"

Slater had to chuckle. Andy didn't like to be watched. "I'm going out of town. I'm not sure for how long. I came over last night to tell you."

"That was romantic of you."

"It's not that kind of gesture," Slater said, sitting up. "It's more of a heads-up type deal."

Andy pulled off his gauntlets and turned toward him. "You don't have to invest … emotionally with me. That means you also don't have to deny … your emotions with me."

"I'm here a lot. I don't want you to get the

wrong idea."

"Have I ever made … demands of you?"

"Never."

"So we're on the same page. You don't want to define this"—Andy gestured in a circle between them—"and I'm OK with that."

Slater rose and found his shirt, pulling it on, and then stepped into his jeans. "You're not going to shanghai me one day and ask me to get married?"

"If there were any chance that might work, I'd jump on it," Andy said, watching him get dressed. "But it's not where we're at."

He faced Andy and put his hands on his hips. "You'd jump on it."

"I like you, Slater, and for some reason I'm able to tolerate your bullshit."

"That sounds like an emotional investment."

"Spending as much time together as we … do, of course we're emotionally involved. We're bonded. I know you feel it too. There's no way we couldn't be."

Slater could feel his heart pounding, felt a lump in his throat. What was that about? It made no freaking sense. "I'm done with romance."

"I know you are. But you can't just switch off how you feel, or drown it in cheap bourbon."

He scoffed. "You always buy me the good stuff."

Andy got up from his chair and stepped closer to him. "Love without pain is impossible," he said, holding his gaze. He thumped Slater's chest with the heel of his palm. "Impossible."

He put his hands on Andy's waist, pulling him closer, and spoke softly. "Why do you do this to me?"

Andy kissed him then, not for long, and pulled away. "I've got work to do."

Slater tied his boots before he said good-bye and went down to the parking lot, where the attendant made him pay the day rate before he left. His apartment wasn't far away, across the 110 freeway in gritty Westlake.

The neighborhood had mostly escaped the waves of gentrification that had shaken up other central parts of the city, probably because it was already too densely built up to make room for McMansions. The streets were pocked with the hallmarks of poverty—fast-food chains, predatory pay-day lenders, dollar stores.

Nosing the Thunderbird into his alley, Slater waited for the garage door to roll up. The best thing about this apartment was the private garage, an unheard-of feature in this neighborhood. He pulled in and killed the engine, made sure the door rolled down all the way, then trotted up the two flights of stairs to his apartment.

It was essentially one big room, with a kitchen

counter near the front door, and a bedroom off the side. The carpet was worn and stained beyond saving, the windows were filmy with decades of dust, and the dingy paint should have been redone ages ago. But it was cheap, and central, and it had that garage.

In the bedroom he found the low futon unmade, dirty clothes strewn on the floor. Rosa, the woman he paid to do his laundry and the futile labor of cleaning the place, hadn't been by in a while. He changed into a clean shirt and kicked the scattered clothes into the bottom of the closet.

His canvas satchel was in the living room, and he stuffed his laptop into it, along with some skivvies and a clean shirt, his toothbrush, and a pint bottle of bourbon. That would last him for an evening, at least, and after that, there had to be liquor stores in Barstow. Eyeing his faux leather jacket hanging in the closet, he pulled it out and folded it into the satchel. It was probably hot as hell up there in the Mojave, but after sundown, at any time of year, the desert got cold.

Setting the bag by the door, he stretched out on his thrift-store sofa, not bothering to pull off his boots. Sometime later, his phone buzzed in his pants, and he started awake. It was a text from Max:

Pulling up outside in 5.

Slater got up and slung on his satchel, then went down the stairs and out to the street, past the building's ground-floor tenant, a cell phone store. The gray Challenger with the dark tinted windows rolled up and stopped at the curb, and Slater opened the passenger door, heaving his bag into the backseat. Max was wearing his gray suit without a necktie.

"Two hours and twenty minutes, according to the navigation app," Max said, glancing at his side mirror and pulling into the street.

"Did your cell provider guy send you that map?"

"I forwarded it to you earlier. As of this morning, Jordan is still connected to that tower."

"If it really is Jordan."

"That data profile was so damn specific. It has to be him."

In a few blocks Max merged onto the freeway, crawling along in the stop-and-go traffic.

"It's Saturday," Slater said. "What are all these people doing out here hogging up the roads?"

Max looked over at him. "You are the traffic."

"That sounds kind of New Age."

"It's literally true, though. *You* are the traffic."

"It's your damn car," Slater said flatly, "and you're driving, so *you* are the traffic."

Max laughed, and merged into the next lane.

"So what came up in your window-shade case?"

"Leslie turned out to be a woman. She's the spouse with the money."

"That's always the one who comes to us," Slater said. "Spouse B is a husband, or a wife?"

"Husband. She thinks he's sleeping with someone else, and needs proof of that to invalidate the prenup."

"What a sap. Someone should explain to these people that if you're going to commit to exclusivity, you're supposed to keep it in your pants."

"It's a good thing that people don't," Max said. "We'd be out of business."

"So you've got some surveillance work to do."

"I told her I'd start in a couple days. Once we pin down Jordan, or get sick of looking for him."

"We'll find him."

The traffic sped up once they were through downtown and headed east on the 10. Max had his big meat hooks wrapped around the wheel, staring at the road, and Slater watched the city roll by.

"Here's the 15 already," Max muttered, and shoulder-checked before he changed lanes.

"Use lane 5," Slater said. "It splits up here so you can go north."

"Lane 5?" Max said.

"It's the second lane from the right."

"So why wouldn't you call it lane 2?"

"Because lane 2 is the second lane from the left. You always count from the left."

"Who knew?" Max said, and changed lanes again.

"How do you not know that?" Slater demanded.

"I guess I don't spend as much time on the road as you do. Plus I never dated a cop."

Headed north out of the metropolis, they wound through the Cajon Pass and into the high desert. Once the road straightened out again, Slater reached into the back for his bag and pulled out his laptop, then found the cell map that Max had sent him.

"This tower covers a lot of ground," Slater said, studying it. "Lots and lots of houses. We won't be able to go door to door."

"There must be some way to smoke him out."

"It looks like there's only one retail boulevard in this zone." He zoomed in and enumerated the businesses. "Liquor store, tire shop, a whole bunch of fast food."

"Is one of them a taco joint? We know that's his preference 46 percent of the time."

"There is a chain taco place," Slater said.

"So let's start there."

Once they were off the freeway, Slater directed him to the commercial strip, and they got a better look at the hot dusty town.

"This was part of Route 66," Max said, pointing to a road sign. "I guess that explains why everything looks overdue for a renovation."

Slater watched for a minute as the widely spaced businesses rolled by. For some reason palm trees had been planted here and there along the boulevard. Those had never been native to this parched corner of the Mojave. Some of the low-rise structures were modern, but many dated to a time before the freeways, and had sagging eaves and ancient bleached paint.

Looking at his screen, Slater said, "The cell zone starts about here."

"Right at the Casa Eleganza motel."

A few minutes of cruising later, Slater said, "That's the end of it."

Max sighed. "At the credit union. That's a lot of ground."

"Let's go check out the taco place. It was right in the middle."

He made a U-turn and drove back the way they'd come, pulling into the dusty lot beside the eatery. The digital sign on the bank up the street said 92°F, and Slater braced himself for a furnace blast, but when he climbed out, the desert air felt dry but not all that hot. The warmth of the sun on his face actually felt good.

The place was deserted when they went in, save for the staff, and they sat where they had a view of the door to eat.

Once he'd finished, Max crumpled up his wrappers. "So what do we do?"

"I say we stake out this place. If we pick the right spot, we can watch the burger joint across the street at the same time."

Back outside, the Challenger was oven-hot when they opened the doors, and Max blasted the air-conditioning before he drove out onto the street. In a half block he made a U-turn, and pulled to the curb, but left the engine idling to power the cool air.

"We're not going to look like stalkers, at least," Max said.

He was right, Slater saw, as there were other vehicles parked on both sides of the boulevard, and the dark car wouldn't stand out.

Max reached into the backseat and produced a set of binoculars. He held them to his eyes and surveyed the taco joint, then shifted to the burger place across the street.

"Part of the parking lot is obscured," he said, and handed them to Slater.

Studying the front door of the burger place

through the glasses, he watched as a woman stepped outside. He could clearly see her facial features, the tuft of hair pulled back with a blue elastic—it would be easy to identify Jordan if he showed up.

"I think this is as good a vantage point as we'll get," Slater said, and handed the binoculars back.

Only a handful of people came and went from either of the junk-food places, and Max intermittently held up the glasses to look at people in the cars that went by in the sparse traffic. Stakeouts were inevitably boring; that's just the way it was. At one point Slater noticed Max's breathing had become louder. Looking over at him, Max was asleep, his head lolling on the headrest. Slater didn't bother him. He'd take a turn himself later.

When Max woke up, he smacked his lips and looked around. Slater handed him the binoculars, and he studied the street for a while.

"Even the trees look dusty and dried out."

"Let me see," Slater said, and took the glasses, aiming them where Max had been looking until he found the tree in the distance, at the edge of an empty lot. "I think it's a red willow. Definitely some kind of *Salix*."

"Is that a desert tree?"

"Technically. I wouldn't have planted it here— they still need water. At least it's native, unlike the freaking washingtonias and the blue palms."

"How do you know all the names? I thought horticulture was about expending elbow grease under the hot sun."

"Doris had the same idea," Slater said. "Manual labor was supposed to keep me out of trouble. Before that, in middle school, she got me into wrestling to work out my aggression. But there's more to horticulture than yard work. I spent lots of time in a classroom."

"Still, I'm surprised that you retain it."

"It doesn't change much over time. Plus plants don't dick around. Give them sunlight and the right conditions, and they thrive."

"Unlike people," Max said. "Do right by them, and they jump bail and go into hiding."

"Yup."

The shadows grew longer as the evening approached, and more vehicles were pulling into the lots of both junk-food outlets, keeping them busier as they traded the glasses, assessing the people as they walked from their cars.

"What about this guy?" Slater said, watching a tall man walk into the burger joint. He handed the glasses to Max. "He's inside now. Wearing a gray track suit."

Max watched intently for a minute as Slater kept an eye on the taco place. Finally he spoke.

"He just stepped out. Jordan isn't that tall, and he's thicker."

Eventually Max passed him the glasses again. A guy wearing black basketball shorts approached the taco joint on foot. Despite the heat he wore a black hoodie over the shaggy mass of his hair. But he was walking right toward them, and his face was visible. He looked to be in his twenties.

"Check out this guy," Slater said, handing him the binoculars.

Max looked toward the taco place. "That's him," he said intently, and sat up, leaning on the steering wheel.

"So your cell provider guy was right."

Max dropped the glasses after Jordan went inside, then cackled, a big goofy smile on his face. "We did it."

"With a little help from that data profile." Slater took the glasses and aimed them at the eatery, but he couldn't see through the glare on the big windows.

"Where did he come from?"

"I caught sight of him this side of the dollar store. He wouldn't have parked over there, so I'm thinking he's on foot."

"So we can tail him. Hopefully he'll lead us back to where he's staying."

"I'll tail him," Slater said. "He doesn't know me, and I look blue-collar, like most of the people around here."

A few minutes later, Jordan came out of the

restaurant. His face was obscured by the hoodie, but it didn't matter—they'd already made him. A white plastic bag dangled from one hand, and he walked back the way he'd come. Slater climbed out and stretched, watching as a teenager rode by on a bicycle. Now that the heat of the day had passed there actually were a few people out on foot.

He'd given him enough lead time, Slater decided, and walked after him. Jordan disappeared at the next side street, past the dollar store. When he rounded the corner, Slater caught sight of him ahead. A couple of blocks farther along, Jordan turned again, and Slater quickened his pace, afraid he might lose him.

A lone pickup rolled by, but no one else was on the street, and as he narrowed the distance between them, Slater pulled out his phone, tilting his head down, as if he were reading something on the screen.

Jordan walked into the driveway of a little bungalow, past the car parked there, not looking back, probably thinking only about his dinner, and went inside. Slater could easily find the place again, but as he walked by, he surreptitiously snapped a photo of the rear plate of the SUV in the driveway, then took several photos of the house, holding the phone down by his waist and not looking at it, not breaking his stride.

Once he was farther up the block, he looked at a map on his phone, zooming in on the satellite view of the neighborhood. There was no alley behind the house, and from what he'd seen, there were only two doors—one on the fenced-in gravel front yard, and one farther back on the driveway.

The last of the sun was fading to twilight as Slater circled the block and headed back to the commercial strip. Climbing into the Challenger, he told Max what he'd seen.

"The place has two doors," Slater said, "and there's two of us. Let's go get him."

"He can't be alone, right? It's getting dark. If we wait till first light, it'll be easier to assess who's there, and harder for him to bail."

"What if he leaves before morning?"

"He's been there for days," Max said. "I don't think he's going anywhere."

"I guess it would be better to drive to Vegas in the daylight too."

"So we'll hit him at sunup."

"I got the tag of the car in the driveway," Slater said, looking at his phone. He pulled up the photos he'd taken of the house and handed it to Max.

"Jordan didn't drive to the taco joint. The car must belong to whoever he's staying with."

"If he's at work tonight, I can get Conrad to run the plate."

"So I guess we need a motel."

"We passed Casa Eleganza on the way in. I'm sure there are others too."

"I want to stay there just because of the name," Max said. He dropped the transmission into gear and pulled into the street.

Casa Eleganza was two floors of motel rooms fronting a parking lot. The building was painted smoky pink, and each of the doors was turquoise. Max pulled up in front of the office and climbed out, taking a minute to stretch before they went in to the desk.

"Are we bunking together?" Max said.

"Naw, man—two rooms."

The clerk nodded and swiped his credit card. "One's upstairs, and one's down."

"Dibs on the upstairs," Max said.

Once they had the keys, they grabbed their bags from the car and went to Slater's room, a few doors down from the office.

"Pure *eleganza*," Max said, stepping inside after Slater and looking around.

It wasn't, not even a little, although it was clean, and the curtains covered the window.

"I'm going to shower," Max said. "You have to find us dinner since you're the high-maintenance vegan."

After he was gone, Slater stretched out on the bed and opened the tracking app to check on his idiot ex-boyfriend, Conrad. When they'd been together, when things had still been good, he'd managed to install a hidden tracker on the moron's phone. It wasn't stalking, not really—he was completely over the dumb-ass, but he needed to keep track of him. Conrad was a cop, and had access to juicy databases and other resources that Slater needed. Plus it was his own fault for letting Slater see the code to unlock his phone.

It took a second for the map to come up, with the green dot in the middle showing where Conrad was. The streets didn't look familiar. Slater zoomed out. Dick-smack was in Manhattan, on the Lower East Side. What the hell was he doing there? Normally Conrad's idea of fun was playing video games, and he never got off his sofa except to go to work, or sometimes to hang out in cruisy dance bars, hitting on guys. Sweaty, buff, fresh-faced guys, drinking and flirting, pulling their shirts off. Fuck Conrad. It was too irritating even to think about, and he killed the app.

Slater spent a minute looking for food options in town, and eventually set the phone face-down on his chest and closed his eyes.

A sharp knock at the door brought him back to consciousness. Outside the peephole he saw Max, still wearing his suit jacket, so he stepped outside.

40

"Chinese, or Mr. Souvlaki," Slater said, pulling the door closed behind him.

Max frowned. "Is that Greek? Let's do Chinese."

FOUR

fter they'd eaten, Max pulled into the motel parking lot and spent a second tapping at his phone.

"Sunrise is at 5:40," he said. "We'll leave here at 5:30."

"Just knock on my door," Slater said, and climbed out.

"You could meet me in the breakfast room."

"It's open that early?"

"The clerk said it started at five."

Once he was alone in his room, Slater flipped open his satchel and found the pint of bourbon, taking a sip and relishing the sharp burn. He screwed the cap back on and stood there for a while, looking at the room. Considering what time he had to be up in the morning, he should probably just go to sleep. He dropped the bottle back in his satchel, burying it under his clean shirt, then tucked his room key into his jeans and pulled on his fake leather jacket.

He hated that it looked like leather, but he liked the way guys looked at him when he was wearing it. Pulling the door closed behind him, he walked past the motel office and out to the street. In the next block was a bar that he'd noticed earlier, low-slung and rustic from out front, the neon in the windows advertising beer and billiards.

It was busy inside, given how small the town was, and there was a lot of denim, and boots, and ball caps. Loud conversations fought to be heard over the twangy country music. The patrons were mostly sitting around the tables, and Slater went to the bar and found an open stool.

The woman tending bar wore a straw cowboy hat and a tank top, revealing her sunbaked cleavage as she leaned toward him.

"A double tequila shot, and a small of whatever's on tap," he said.

She nodded and stepped away, and Slater twisted around to survey the room. Back in LA, even in a dive bar, most of the urban patrons would be polished and plucked and sculpted. Here the men and women alike were manual laborers and desert rats, with little artifice—hair left to gray naturally and grow the way it wanted, faces deeply lined by the sun.

"Eight-fifty," the bartender said, setting the shot glass and the beer in front of him. Slater had to smile at how cheap it was, and found a sawbuck in his pocket.

"Keep it," he said, sliding it across the counter.

She flashed him a smile and scooped it up as she stepped away.

Under his revised booze rules, he wasn't supposed to be drinking alone, unless it was just the one. When he was with people, he was allowed to have more. But this place was full of people, technically, so maybe that was close enough.

Picking up the shot glass, he slammed the tequila, coughing a little as it burned his throat. She'd poured him a generous double, and this stuff was strong, the flavor smoky. That warm familiar feeling grew in his belly and spread— contentment, and the world slowing down, like coming home again. He smiled to himself and sipped his beer.

A guy stepped up beside him and leaned over the vacant stool, bracing himself with his palms on the bar and nodding to catch the bartender's eye. As he ordered, Slater looked over the contours of his snug jeans, his tanned forearms, the little paunch over his belt. Totally fuckable, he decided.

The guy looked at him sidelong, and when

Slater didn't look away, he demanded, "What?"

Slater swiveled sideways and put an elbow on the bar. "Just admiring the scenery."

"You were looking at my ass."

"Admiring it. I just said that."

"Dude," he said, frowning, "I'm straight."

"Is that why you're wearing those fuck-me boots? So that I won't hit on you?"

He lifted his foot to glance at one of his scuffed and dusty work boots, as if he might have missed something, then paid for his beer, eyeing Slater again before he walked away.

There weren't really many prospects in here, Slater decided, surveying the room again. He drained his beer glass and walked back to the motel, where he pulled off his boots and stretched out on the bed.

The hookup app was a lot less work than trolling a damn bar, and when he opened it, he was surprised at how many guys were on the make in this small town. Half of them had no face pic, but swiping through the options, he found one with a great bushy mustache and messaged him:

I want to fuck you. My place. No drugs.

It didn't take long to get a reply:

Where's your place?

Slater texted him the name of the motel and

his room number, then got up and pulled his shirt off, revealing his tight white undershirt. It always seemed to make a good first impression with guys.

Soon after came a knock at the door. When Slater pulled it open, the guy flashed a smile, his face red with embarrassment.

"You look just like your profile pic."

"And you trimmed your mustache," Slater said.

"It was getting itchy. I hope that's not a deal breaker."

Slater stepped aside so he could come in.

"I'm Glen," the guy said, looking around. "I haven't been inside this place. It's not too bad. I drive by all the time. I work for the railroad ..."

His voice trailed off as Slater stepped in front of him and looked him in the eye. Moving closer, he put his hands on Glen's waist, then kissed him, exploring what was left of his mustache. His mouth was taught and warm, and even better, getting up in his grill precluded the yapping.

Leaning into him, he could feel Glen's stiff cock. Slater pulled him to the bed, where he sat down and buried his nose in his crotch. Glen gasped and unbuckled his belt, dropping his jeans, and he let Slater nuzzle him for a moment before he climbed onto the bed. Kneeling behind Slater, he reached around and ran his hands over his chest, then pulled off Slater's undershirt, and spent a minute exploring his skin.

"Come here," Glen said, and shifted up to make room for him.

Slater stretched out on his back, and Glen unbuckled his jeans, pulling them down, and then off completely, tossing them onto the floor. He took Slater into his mouth, gently at first and then deeply. The intense sensation made Slater shiver and grab Glen's wiry white hair, but then he got used to it, and lay back, enjoying it. He could feel Glen's mustache, and looked down to watch.

Slater grabbed his hair again to stop him, but it was too late, and he came, arching his back, straining into it.

Glen flopped onto his back, breathing hard. "I guess this means you're not going to fuck me."

"You're just so good at that. I couldn't stop."

"It's OK."

"What are we going to do for you?"

"Do you want to blow me?"

Slater shifted down the bed and grabbed his cock with one hand, exploring between his legs with the other, and took him into his mouth. As he worked a thumb inside him, Glen got more turned on, and soon climaxed, groaning as he came.

Slater rolled onto his back and put an arm

over his eyes, catching his breath in the brief moment of quiet.

"So what are you doing here?" Glen said. "Mostly the people who visit are tourists from the highways. You don't look like a tourist, at least not the kind I usually see. Are you from LA? Are you working up here?"

"I'm on a silent retreat," Slater said flatly, not moving his arm.

"Well, that's kind of weird, because you're talking."

"And yet I strive for silence."

"I get that," Glen said, running his hand gently on Slater's belly. "It's nice to unplug once in a while, and get away from work, and the routine, and all that. I don't think I would have come to this town to do that, though. There must be some nice retreat places in the desert. Maybe down in Palm Springs."

Unable to tune him out, Slater got up and went to his satchel, reaching in for the pint bottle of bourbon. After he took a pull, he offered it to Glen, who took a small sip.

"Is that all your luggage? You sure travel light."

"There's a toothbrush in there somewhere." Slater took back the bottle, guzzling from it. Setting it on the bedside table, he lay down again, and Glen shifted closer.

"Is that bourbon? It tasted like decent booze."

"No more talking," Slater said, and killed the lamp, leaving only the ambient light emanating from the bathroom. With his eyes closed, he started to drift off, but woke when Glen got up.

"I'm going to go," he said, and winced at the glare when Slater sat up and clicked on the lamp.

Slater watched him pull on his shirt, then step into his jeans. The handle of an old-fashioned handgun poked out of his front pocket as he buckled his belt.

"Are you packing?" Slater said.

Glen raised his eyebrows. "The pistol?" He pulled it out and deftly popped open the cylinder, then gave it a spin before he snapped it back in place and tucked the weapon away. It looked to be fully loaded. He eyed Slater, his expression earnest. "I usually am. You never know who you're going to meet. There are lots of crazy people around."

"Tell me about it," Slater said flatly.

"So can I get your number? I get down to the big city sometimes. I assume you're from LA, right? You look like you're from LA."

Slater reached down for his jeans and found a business card, then handed it to him.

"Thanks," Glen said, and stood reading it. "Investigator. Wow—is that why you're here? What are you investigating?"

"I really need to get to sleep."

"Right," Glen said, and tucked the card away. A moment later he was gone, and Slater killed the light, luxuriating in the rich silence.

Slater woke in the darkness to the strident alarm on his phone. It took him a minute to figure out where he was, but eventually it clicked, and he turned on the lamp, wincing at the brightness, then washed up and pulled on his jeans and the clean shirt. Lifting his satchel onto his shoulder, he dropped his room key at the front desk and found Max in the breakfast room, wearing his gray suit.

"I can't believe they put food out at this hour," Slater said, looking over the offerings.

"Country folks need to be up early," Max said, wiping his mouth with a napkin. "Have a waffle. They're amazing."

"I'll eat this on the way." He grabbed an apple from the counter and waited while Max drained his mug.

The air outside was cold as they walked to the car. Once they were out on the boulevard, Slater saw the glow of the sun looming below the horizon.

Minutes later they were rolling up on the house that Jordan had gone into. Max drove by slowly to scan the layout. Two vehicles sat in the driveway.

"Was the Neon there last night?"

"Only the SUV," Slater said. "So how athletic is this guy? If he bails out a window, the fence around the backyard is high enough to slow most people down, but not if he does parkour."

"That doesn't sound like Jordan. I bet he'd run for the driveway."

Max parked across the street, a few doors down, and they sat for a minute to discuss their strategy as the dark sky took on the gray of twilight. The front door swung open, and a woman stepped out, wearing black pants and a white shirt, her dark hair bundled up on her head. Slater instinctively slouched lower in his seat. She looked tired, fussing with her keys as she stepped over to the little blue Neon and climbed in behind the wheel.

"Jordan's girlfriend?" Slater said.

"She looks a little old for him. Besides, he already has one in LA."

"Why would that stop him?"

"This guy's not a player."

Exhaust billowed from the back end of the Neon, and a moment later it backed out of the driveway.

"Where's she going at dawn on Sunday morning?" Slater said.

"Church?"

"That outfit, though. I bet she's a security guard."

"I didn't see any insignia," Max said, "but you're right, that was more the vibe. Sometimes those companies make you leave the shield on the jacket, and the jacket stays at work."

"One car left," Slater said.

"So he's probably not alone."

"We should hit him anyway."

"Agreed."

Max pulled his weapon out of its holster and opened the console between the seats, setting it inside. It was a wise move—if this went badly, and law enforcement got involved, it would be so much worse if he was armed.

They climbed out of the car and eased the doors closed so as not to make any sound, and kept silent as they walked up the driveway. Max stepped up to the front door, and Slater hung back, at the corner of the house, to keep an eye on the other exit.

Once Slater was in position, he nodded, and Max pounded on the door, then cocked his head to listen to what was happening inside. He pounded again, and a burly guy in a T-shirt and boxer shorts, sleep in his eyes, pulled it open and scowled at Max. This was no hard-core lowlife—he looked worried. A savvy crook never would have come to the door.

Max threw his weight at the guy, catching him off guard, and shoved him inside. Slater hustled to follow.

"What the hell?" he shouted.

Slater stepped in to find the guy grappling with Max in the space in front of the sofa. Through the archway into the kitchen, he saw Jordan, wearing only a pair of powder-blue boxer shorts, moving fast toward the side door. Slater leapt onto the sofa and hurdled the back, tackling Jordan before he could get the door open. His bare shoulder slammed against the frame, and Slater wrenched him away from the door, shoving him backward. His butt struck the kitchen table, sending it skittering against the wall with a clatter of dishes.

Jordan came at him and tried to throw a punch, but he didn't know how to do it, and Slater easily weaved around his arm and landed a sharp right to his eye. Jordan spun away and yelped, then crouched a little, disoriented by the blow.

Max had freed himself of the big guy, and he stepped in from the living room, breathing hard and adjusting the lapels of his jacket. But he hadn't actually neutralized him—behind Max, suddenly, the big guy appeared, carrying a golf club. He raised it over his shoulder with both hands and took a swing at Max's head.

"Down," Slater shouted, and Max ducked, the club whiffing the air above him.

Slater dodged past Max and punched the guy in his flabby gut, then wrenched the club out of his hand as he buckled over, and landed a head-snapping blow to his chin. Slater tossed the club to the carpet and kicked him in the ribs as he went down.

"Why do you make me do this to you?" Slater shouted, and kicked him again, a solid blow to the kidney.

"Enough," Max said sharply.

Slater glanced at him, furious at being interrupted, and then looked back at the guy on the floor, immobile now. Struggling to quell his rage, he resisted the urge to kick him again, and took a step back. He ran a hand through his hair.

Next to Max, Jordan stood staring at him, eyes wide. Max had his right arm twisted up behind his back. The guy had a nice body, with definition in his chest, and that great head of hair with the little twists in it. He was darker than Vanessa, but there was a family resemblance, maybe, around the eyes. Behind them on the kitchen floor was a puddle of milk, and bits of breakfast cereal, and the overturned bowl they'd knocked off the table.

Regaining his composure, Jordan tried to pull away from Max, who twisted his wrist and elbow more tightly into his back. Jordan winced and stopped struggling.

"I'm calling the cops," he snapped.

"Fine with me," Max said. "They'll be happy to make the arrest."

Jordan glared at him sidelong, his upper lip curling into a sneer. Max frog-marched him into the living room, past the crumpled form of the other man, and shoved him down into an easy chair.

"Where's your phone?" Max demanded.

Jordan rubbed his injured eye and mumbled, "I don't know."

"If I have to hunt for it," Max said sharply, "I'm going to coldcock you, like your friend over there."

Jordan met his gaze. "It's beside the bed."

Max eyed Slater, who walked through the kitchen to find the bedrooms. Despite his flabbiness, and his usual crutch of carrying a weapon, Max could actually handle the rough stuff when he needed to, Slater thought. The smaller room had a single bed in it, unmade and with the covers shoved to one side. A cell phone sat on the night-stand. Slater snatched it up and took it to Max, who tucked it into his suit pocket.

Max had positioned himself between Jordan and the front door, and Slater instinctively stood near the archway into the kitchen.

"You can't make me go to Vegas," Jordan said. "You can't keep me here either. That's kidnap-ping."

"You're a fugitive from justice," Max said. "I'm acting as an officer of the court."

"Can you do that?" he demanded.

"I can until the cops get here, if that's how you want to play it. If you think about it, though, the trip to Vegas would be a lot more comfortable in my car than handcuffed to a bench in the back of a prisoner transport van."

"Why are you after me?" Jordan said, his eyes narrowing. "As a favor to Vanessa? You have to know that she's not really into you. This isn't going to impress her."

"It wasn't just her money that you forfeited when you missed your arraignment. It was mine too."

"The whole thing was a frame-up," Jordan said, raising his voice and waving a hand.

"You said that before," Max said. "I don't want to hear it. You do need to convince me, however, that we're going to have an uneventful ride to

Vegas. Otherwise the cuffs go on now."

Jordan glared at Slater. "The fuck are you?"

Slater put his hands on his hips and jutted his chin. "I'm the guy who just punched you in the face."

Max chuckled. "Slater's my business partner. He's my backup today."

"Are you a PI too?"

Slater ignored the question, but Jordan sat up in the easy chair, leaning toward him.

"Maybe you can talk some sense into your thick friend here. Listen to my side of it."

"When you jump bail, there's only one side," Slater said. "It's called a bench warrant."

Jordan looked away and slumped back. As they watched, he closed his eyes for a moment and took a deep breath. When he opened them again, the fire was gone, his anger fading. It was as if he was willing himself to be calm. It was a smart decision, Slater thought, watching the transformation—accepting defeat and dropping the belligerence would make the rest of the day a lot less painful for him.

"I do feel bad about your money," Jordan said quietly. "I guess I should have known I wouldn't get very far. I'll go back to Vegas with you. No handcuffs required."

Max looked at Slater. "If he runs, can you catch him? I won't be able to."

"Maybe," Slater said, eyeing Jordan. "He's pretty fit."

"I guess it doesn't really matter—I've got my sidearm." Looking to Jordan, he added, "I'll aim for your legs. You probably won't die, unless I hit an artery."

Jordan huffed and looked at the unconscious man on the floor.

"We should go," Slater said.

"Can I put some clothes on first?" Jordan demanded.

Max waved an arm, and followed him through the kitchen into the bedroom. Slater stood in the doorway to watch. Jordan picked up his pants, and Max took them from him, checking the pockets. He pulled out a vape pen and examined it briefly, then threw it into the corner of the room, where it hit the wall behind the bed with a *crack*. The wallet went into Max's jacket, then he handed the pants back, and they both watched as Jordan got dressed.

"If you have to pee, go now," Max said. "We won't be stopping."

Jordan stepped into the bathroom and tried to close the door, scowling at Max when he shoved it open and stood in the doorway.

The big guy was stirring now, Slater saw, stepping past him into the living room.

"Is your host aware that you're on the lam?"

Max said, following Jordan toward the front door.

"Why does that matter?"

"I need to know whether he's going to call the cops and say, 'Oh, poor me, these bullies came into my house and punched me.'"

Jordan sighed. "He knows what's up."

"Good," Max said, and eyed the man on the floor. "He's taking his time to come around. I guess we'll do it with a voice mail." Max pulled Jordan's phone out of his jacket pocket and held it out for him. "Unlock it." Jordan did, and Max pulled the phone back. "What's his name?"

"He's under 'Willy.'"

"Here's what you're going to say," Max said, reciting the words as he swiped at the phone. From the back of the house came the faint sound of a cell phone ringing, and when it stopped, Willy's voice-mail greeting played on Jordan's phone, rattling the tinny speaker. Max held it up for Jordan to talk.

"I'm leaving today of my own free will," Jordan said, repeating Max's words. "I encourage you not to report this morning's visitors. If you do, they will make sure you're charged with harboring a fugitive. That's a felony."

Max ended the call and slipped the phone into his jacket, then eyed Slater. "Can you handle him until we get into the car?"

Slater grabbed the back of Jordan's shirt

collar, and even though the guy seemed resigned to acquiescing, he gave it a tug to make sure he knew that he had a firm grip. Stepping out the front door, Max glanced around the empty street, then waved for Slater to follow.

Slater pulled the door closed and walked out to the Challenger, watching as Max opened the passenger door and reached in to grab his weapon from the console. Standing erect again, he opened his jacket and holstered it.

"If you'd brought that inside, you wouldn't have had to deck Willy," Jordan said.

"If I'd brought it inside, I'd be a felonious lowlife like you." He gestured and said, "Get in."

Slater walked him to the passenger door and stood over him as he sat down and buckled the seatbelt.

"Can you drive?" Max said. "I'll sit behind him and keep my weapon handy."

SIX

Slater climbed in behind the wheel and started the engine, then shifted the seat and adjusted the mirrors before he pulled into the street. It was amazing how smooth these new cars felt, how gentle the ride was.

Jordan looked over at him as he navigated out to the boulevard. "He calls me a felonious lowlife, but you're the one who beat the shit out of Willy. You were on him even after he was unconscious."

Slater ignored that, braking for a red light. He could feel Jordan's eyes on him.

"You're the devil," Jordan said intently.

Slater sighed. "I've heard that one before."

"How are you not in jail?" Jordan demanded, raising his voice.

"Settle down," Max said, and tapped him on the shoulder.

"You don't know what I've done, or where I've been," Slater said, glancing at him with a frown.

"You've served time?"

"Not serious time."

Jordan stared at the road for a while before he spoke. "I'm not the one who should be getting locked up."

Slater accelerated down the ramp onto the 15, punching it to merge in front of a slow-moving semi.

"Damn, this thing is quiet," he said, eyeing Max in the rearview.

"That's because it's not forty years old."

They rode in silence for a while, past the Calico Mountains and into the expansive Mojave flatlands. Jordan sat with his arms folded, staring out the window.

"You've got a captive audience for a couple of hours," Slater said finally. "You said you wanted to tell us your side of it."

Jordan looked at him. "Seriously?"

"It's either that or NPR."

"I was framed," he said intently.

"You said that part already."

"Right. So this guy asked me to go pick up a statue."

"There's always a guy," Max said flatly, and

rolled his eyes when Slater glanced at him in the rearview. "I've heard a thousand versions of this story from a thousand deadbeats."

"Just hear me out," Jordan said. "His name is Thiago. He said he was Argentinean. Not the European kind—the Latin kind, like you." He eyed Slater. "Dude is a medical doctor. Dresses all slick and money. I owed him a favor."

"For doing what?" Slater said, checking the side mirror as he pulled out to pass a semitrailer.

"I owed him a couple grand," Jordan said. "Not for anything shady. I just didn't have that kind of cash, so I agreed to work it off. He gave me that gun, and he told me to go to Vegas. I was supposed to get the statue from a woman's office. She's a doctor too."

"What's her name?"

"Paola Martín. She has a little practice in a strip mall."

"If you were just doing this Thiago guy a favor," Slater said, "why did you need a weapon? Why not just go in and ask for it?"

"He said the statue was his, and he could prove it with paperwork, but that she wouldn't give it up. His only other option was to sue her, and that would take months. He told me to go in the morning because the office would be closed. I was supposed to break in the back door and grab it."

"So what was the heater for?" Slater demanded.

"Thiago said it was just in case. He gave me a tool to open the door on the alley, but when I got there, it wasn't locked. It wasn't bolted, I mean—the handle was locked, but I was able to push in the latch with the tip of the tool, and then open the door. So I didn't even break anything."

"What kind of tool?"

"Metal, about this long," Jordan said, and held out his hands. "One of those things for working on cars."

"A tire iron," Slater said.

"Not for tires. One end of it was curved, with a notch in it, for pulling out nails."

"That's a jimmy."

"That's not what he called it."

"A crowbar," Max offered.

"That's it," Jordan said, and snapped his fingers. "He gave me a crowbar."

Slater eyed Max in the rearview and raised his eyebrows. Was this guy really that clueless? Max just pursed his lips and shrugged.

"So you went inside," Slater said, "and waved the gun around?"

"Not right away. I didn't expect there to be people inside. Paola was there, and I told her what I wanted, and she laughed in my face. She said, 'Tell Thiago to go fuck himself.'"

"Then you pulled the gun."

"Right. She had the statue in the bottom of

a cupboard. I took it and left. Nobody got hurt."

"What kind of statue was it?"

"About this tall," he said, and held his hand at chin level. "Thiago said it was a statue of the Buddha. What Paola pulled out of her cupboard was a statue of Guanyin. I thought it was the wrong thing, that she was messing with me, but she insisted it was the one Thiago wanted. He told me some story about how attached he was to it, but that was garbage. He didn't even know what it was."

"Who's Guanyin?" Max said, leaning between the seats.

"She's like a goddess," Jordan said, "although Buddhists don't really do gods. Guanyin is on the path of enlightenment, but she's not there yet. Sometimes she's called the goddess of mercy."

"How do you know all that?"

"Our parents dabbled in Buddhism. Vanessa never told you that?"

"Maybe she did," Max said. "There's some Buddhist paraphernalia around her place. That stone head with the knobbly hair."

"So you brought it back to LA?" Slater said.

"I took it to Thiago's office. It was the right statue. He was pretty happy to see it, but he wouldn't take his piece back, and he gave me the bum's rush. That was my big mistake—not leaving the gun there."

"Because the cops found it."

"Apparently someone at the clinic in Vegas followed me into the alley and wrote down my plate number. So it was just a matter of time."

"Usually people who are planning an armed robbery take the time to steal a car first," Max said.

Jordan scowled at him. "I have a college degree. I'm not that kind of people."

"That's not how the Clark County DA sees things," Max said, and sat back.

"Where did you go when you got bailed out?" Slater said.

"Back to LA first. When I missed the court date, I went to Bardo."

"Why were you in Barstow?" Max said. "Whose house was that?"

"Willy's. That's the guy you attacked."

"Defended myself against," Slater said flatly. "It's called self-defense."

Jordan scoffed. "Willy is sort of a cousin. We used to stop in there on the way to Vegas when we were kids."

"Great," Max said. "More 'splaining I'll have to do to Vanessa."

"Who was the woman who left earlier in the blue Neon?" Slater said.

"Willy's girlfriend. She works at Bardo College."

"Why do you pronounce it like that?" Slater said. "I've only heard it as *bar-stow*."

Jordan chuckled. "In Buddhism, *bardo* is the place you go between two lives, when your consciousness isn't in a body. Barstow is kind of like that—it's in the intermediary space between LA and Vegas."

"I can't believe you know that," Max said.

Turning to scowl at him, Jordan said, "You judgmental ass. Why wouldn't I?"

"You heard that in a class? Or because your parents were kinda-sorta Buddhists?"

"It's not really esoteric knowledge. The *bardo* is what the *Tibetan Book of the Dead* is all about. You might have heard of it if you'd ever picked up a book."

"I'll have to ask Vanessa about that."

Jordan waved dismissively. "Think about the symbolism of it. In that liminal place, as a pure soul, you're supposed to have these peaceful transformative experiences, expanding your awareness, moving out of one incarnation and preparing for the next. And you two goons went in and started a fight."

"If that reincarnation jazz is for real," Max said, "I would hope you'd get to rest between lives. Like, get some sleep, maybe, or a beach vacation. Something with mai tais."

"If there are other people in your liminal

state," Slater said, "there's always going to be a need for fisticuffs."

Jordan studied him. "That's a dark outlook."

"Dark, but realistic. And speaking of dark, I'm not the one who robbed a doctor's office."

"You are the one, though, who broke into Willy's house and started a fight."

"He let us in," Max said. "There was no housebreaking."

"It was more than a fight," Slater said. "It was a brawl."

"What's the difference?"

"It's about the number of participants. A fight is two people, and a brawl is more than two. It's what the French call a *rififi,* or in Russian, an *ulichnaya draka.*"

"Do you speak either of those languages?"

"Not a word."

"Slater is something of a savant about violence," Max said.

"Yeah, and I have the bruises to prove it."

"That was your own doing," Slater said. "You shouldn't have tried to hit me."

Jordan sighed and looked out the window, and they rode in silence for a while. Traffic had picked up, and Slater kept pace with the flow in the left lane.

After a while, Jordan spoke. "So how did you two become partners?"

"Slater gave me a monumental beatdown," Max said. "Worse than what Willy got. In fairness, though, I did try to crown him with a shovel."

"Technically, it was a spade," Slater said. "But that's how I remember it too."

"Weren't you mad at each other? How did you become friends after that?"

"It's not about being friends," Max said. "It's about establishing trust. I was working for a crook, and Slater convinced me to step away from that. Away from the dark side."

"You didn't know the extent of what that guy was up to," Slater said.

"Yeah, he was bad news. Anyway, when you're caught up in a bad situation—a crisis—you can see a person's true colors. All the bullshit recedes, and you know what they're really all about. That's the foundation of trust."

It was an eloquent way to explain it, Slater thought, eyeing him in the rearview mirror. Maybe that's why it was easy to be around Max. He did trust him, and it was a neutral experience—he didn't want to fuck him, and most of the time he didn't want to punch him in the face either.

"How did you get with my sister?" Jordan said.

"That was an incredible gift from the universe.

The heavens opened, there was harp music, and Aphrodite smiled down on me for some reason."

"OK," Jordan said flatly. "Who made the first move?"

"I guess I did. I met her in a coffee place, and I gave her a hard time about the silly drink she ordered. And she flirted back."

"I could never figure it out," he said. "You don't seem like her type."

"Because I'm white?"

"Because you're older than her, and dumber, and working-class. Our parents were intellectuals."

Max scoffed. "You're in no position to judge my intelligence. Whatever it is that she sees in me, I know I'm a very lucky man."

"That's a good perspective to have," Jordan said. "Maybe it means you'll treat her right."

"What do you think, Slater?" Max eyed him in the mirror. "Should I be taking relationship advice from a guy who robbed a doctor at gunpoint?"

Slater chuckled at that and focused on the road.

As they got closer to Las Vegas, the highway ran across a landscape dotted with Joshua trees, their spiky branches jutting at odd angles. A while later they passed the massive solar plants in the hazy distance at Tonopah. Worthy of science fiction, their collector towers glowed as bright as the sun.

"Can I have my phone?" Jordan said. "I want to call my girlfriend before I go back to jail."

"I'll dial," Max said, and held the phone out for Jordan to unlock. When he'd initiated the call, he handed it to Jordan.

"I wish you'd picked up," Jordan said quietly into the phone. "I won't see you for a while. Love you, baby girl."

Max took it back from him and then pulled out his own. Tapping at it, he held it to his ear.

"Hey, man … I need to drop someone with a warrant. Which station up there would be the least amount of trouble? … OK … It's Sunday— will they keep him there?" Max listened for a moment, then ended the call and eyed Slater. "I found the gentlest police station in Las Vegas. Let me put it in your navigation."

Slater handed him his phone, and took it back a minute later, setting it in the mount on the dash. According to the screen, the drive time from here was less than half an hour.

SEVEN

The police station was dead quiet when they rolled up. Slater climbed out and stretched. It was hot already, and the air here felt different, even from Barstow—thinner, maybe, and the daylight felt brighter. Max climbed out and pulled off his jacket, then undid his holster and put it in the trunk. It was a lot easier to ditch it than to explain to the cops that he was armed.

When Jordan climbed out, he looked apprehensive. Slater walked close behind him as they went inside, just in case he decided to bolt at the last minute. But he didn't, and they stepped into a small lobby. A tack board hung on the wall, plastered with community notices. The only other door was behind the tall desk, where a uniformed cop was parked, a skinny twenty-something guy with the same stupid haircut Conrad wore. He glanced up from his screen as they stepped in.

Max approached the desk and spoke for a minute, then pulled Jordan's wallet out of his jacket and handed the guy a card—Jordan's ID.

Standing back a ways with their charge, Slater could see the concern in Jordan's eyes, the sweat beading his brow.

"How long ago were you supposed to show for your arraignment?" Slater asked him, keeping his voice low.

"It's been four days."

"That's not too bad. It gets worse the longer you delay it. When you do get arraigned, go in with a lawyer. They might be able to come up with a plausible excuse."

He sighed. "I don't really have the resources for anything like that at this point in my life."

"Vanessa does."

"She's not going to help me now. I ripped her off. Demonstrated that I'm a felonious lowlife."

"You might be surprised what she'd do," Slater said. "If she bought in to any of that Buddhist stuff, I'm sure she knows that nobody is beyond redemption."

Jordan eyed him sidelong. "That sounds like something you hope is true."

"What was the doctor's name? The one in LA."

"Thiago Sobel. His office is in Beverly Hills. Why?"

"I might go ask him about the Guanyin statue."

"Why would you do that? Max is convinced I'm lying."

"I'm sure you probably are," Slater said. "It's what most people do most of the time. But something feels hinky."

"Ask Thiago why he wanted it so bad when he doesn't even know what it is," Jordan said intently. "He thought it was the Buddha, but it's not. And ask him where he got that gun. It had no serial number—that multiplied my misery here significantly."

"No promises," Slater said, gesturing dismissively. "Listen, when you're on the inside, be honest about why you're there. You don't have to admit to anything, but you have to get into it if anyone asks."

Jordan frowned. "Why?"

"If you don't talk about it, people assume you're a chomo."

"What's that?"

"A sex offender. They won't treat you very well."

The cop at the desk stood up and called to Jordan, "You jumped bail."

"I just told you that," Max said, and absently set Jordan's phone and wallet up on the desk. "But

I guess if it's in the computer, it must be true."

Another uniformed cop stepped out from the back and fixed Jordan with an intent gaze.

"He's surrendering himself willingly," Max said, raising his voice, watching him step around the desk toward Jordan.

"Here we go," Jordan muttered.

"Show him your hands," Slater said.

At least he hadn't drawn his weapon. Slater turned and went outside, squinting in the bright daylight. He didn't need to watch it happening. Max came out a minute later, his expression grim.

"I feel bad for the kid, in a way," Max said, stepping around to the driver's side of the Challenger. "It breaks Vanessa's heart to see him screw up his life."

"You really should get him a lawyer. At least for the arraignment," Slater said, and climbed in the other side.

Max eyed him as he started the engine. "He's going away for at least three years no matter what."

"With a decent lawyer it'll be three and not twenty."

"Maybe if we get the bail money back."

"If Vanessa doesn't have it, use the cash in the safe," Slater said.

"That's mostly yours."

"It's company money. It's ours, and it's meant for stuff like this."

Max sighed and pulled into the street. "My first reaction is to say, let him rot. But I'm sure Vanessa is on the same wavelength as you, all misty-eyed and forgiving."

"I'm not sure I believe anything he says either. But everybody deserves a fair shake."

"We should eat," Max said.

"Not here. Vegas isn't good for guys like us. I'm afraid I'll drown."

"There's no grub between here and Barstow. One meal won't kill you. We'll stay away from the Strip."

"What about that place?" Slater said, pointing out the windshield at a chain diner. "It's even on the right side of the street."

Max pulled into the parking lot. Inside, the place wasn't busy, and they sat at a booth.

"You need menus?" the waitress asked, her tone indifferent, stopping beside their table.

"Thanks for asking, Gwen," Max said, glancing at her name tag and flashing a smile. She had a dozen years on him, and sunken smoker's cheeks, but he couldn't help himself—Max was a flirt. "It would make my day if you brought me a BLT."

"Sure thing, hon." She filled their mugs from her bulbous carafe of java and eyed Slater.

"Oatmeal," he said, "and hold the fixings. An order of fries too."

When the food landed, Max picked up his sandwich and eyed Slater's meal.

"I feel bad that's all there is for you to eat," Max said.

"I'm used to it. It always happens when you leave civilization."

After they'd paid, Max navigated to the 15. Lots of times on Sunday evening there was stop-and-go congestion all the way back to Los Angeles, but it was early enough in the day that the traffic was moving.

They talked about the morning's events, clarifying the details, debating Jordan's credibility. Once they were talked out, Slater watched the arid countryside, gaping as they crossed the expanse of Joshua trees. It was such an unusual species of yucca, grand and eye-catching and absurd at the same time.

Closer to Bardo, he checked Conrad's location on his phone. The moron was still in New York, but the green dot had moved to Brooklyn, close to the waterfront. When he zoomed in, it looked like a row of old warehouses. What the hell was he up to? Slater dialed his number and listened to it ring a few times before Conrad picked up.

"What do you need, Slater?"

"It sounds noisy. Where are you?"

"New York."

"Why?" Slater demanded.

"It's for a cop thing."

"The LAPD has no jurisdiction in Brooklyn. What's his name?"

"How did you know I was in Brooklyn?"

"You said New York. Brooklyn's in New York," he said, thinking quickly. "I'm out of town too—Las Vegas, sucker."

"You hate Vegas," Conrad said.

Slater sighed. It wasn't that he hated the place. He knew that if he got too close, it would pull him under, consume him, bring out his worst self. He'd wind up doing dirty work for lowlifes, becoming one of them instead of hunting them down.

"Can you hear me?" Conrad said.

"When are you back?"

"In a couple of days. What do you need?"

"From you, nothing," Slater said, raising his voice. "So quit bugging me." Before Conrad could reply, he ended the call.

"Everything OK?" Max said, glancing over at him.

"Conrad's in New York. Who does that—gets on a plane and deliberately flies to winter? He's such a freaking idiot."

"What's he doing over there?"

"Probably sleazing around nightclubs, and dancing with his shirt off, and fucking some damn twinky."

"It's a good thing you're over that guy. Otherwise you'd be upset."

Slater eyed him sidelong and spoke in a low voice. "Spread out."

Wisely, Max didn't respond to that. He stifled a laugh and kept his eyes on the road.

The trip back to civilization always seemed longer than the outbound, and Slater was bored before they even got to Bardo. He played with the radio, running through the available stations.

"How do you feel about *ranchera* music?" he said. "That's the station with the best signal."

Max looked in his mirror as he changed lanes. "Is that the kind with all the brass? I guess I can handle that."

Slater let it play for a while, until the signal got staticky, then killed it, and sat with his arms folded, watching the landscape roll by.

———◆———

A few hours later they pulled up in front of Slater's building.

"Thanks for your help, buddy," Max said.

"It goes both ways," Slater said, climbing out and retrieving his satchel from the trunk.

It was much cooler here than in the desert, even though the sun felt just as bright. Upstairs, Slater pulled his boots off and stretched out on the sofa. He felt wiped out, like it should be dark outside already. Looking at his phone, he decided not to open the hookup app. He could take a night off now and then.

The tracking app showed that Conrad was still in Brooklyn. Such a prick. He was probably there to trample some other poor chump's soul into a bloody pulp. Huffing at the thought of it, he killed the app and dropped the phone on the carpet.

Under his revised booze rules, he could have his nightly ration now—he was in for the evening, and he wasn't working later. Rising, he went to the kitchen cupboard and pulled out the almost new fifth, pouring the beautiful amber liquid into a tumbler. Just a half glass. When he slammed it, he paused to close his eyes and feel the burn, savoring the heady fumes in his nose.

On the sofa again, he sank into the golden warmth as it lulled his mind. Max was pissed at Jordan, and rightfully so, but nothing in the guy's story seemed patently bogus. Not many people could be talked into committing armed robbery without mulling the consequences, but it was possible—the depth of human stupidity was unfathomable. Jordan knew all about Guanyin and *The Tibetan Book of the Dead*, but he didn't know the difference between a tire iron and a jimmy, and he hadn't had the sense to ditch that handgun in a storm drain, or toss it in a lake, or even better, leave it on Thiago's desk. It could all be an act, of course, the gullibility, and it was always easier to believe someone who was earnest and good-looking. But maybe the guy really had been played.

Sometime later, when he woke, still on the sofa, the room was dark. He could feel the buzz of the bourbon. He probably should have eaten something. Scrabbling on the carpet for his phone, he checked the time. It was still early. Sex was out; he was too loaded. But he wasn't allowed to drink any more either. Gazing at the dark sky above the building across the street, he listened to the incessant low rumble of the metropolis. Stuff was always happening in this gritty cesspool, day and night. People were always up to something. It was relentless.

There was house music on the radio at this hour, and he turned it on, just loud enough to drown out the city. He was in a weird head space—agitated but torpid. Two days in the desert had worn him out, but he wasn't tired enough to sleep. The glow of the bourbon was fading, and yet the booze rules dictated that he couldn't drink any more.

They really were arbitrary, those rules. He was doing it for Doris and Conrad and Andy anyway, so that they wouldn't pull anything, an intervention or an ambush to get him locked up in rehab or on a psych hold. Why was he living his life for his mother and his drooling slack-jawed ex? Andy never told him what to do, but it was obvious what he thought Slater should do, and it involved sitting around on folding chairs with a bunch of junkies, drinking watery coffee and talking about their higher power.

Fuck it, he decided, and got up. The fifth was waiting for him, inert and nonjudgmental, golden and luminous in the low light. Slater guzzled from the bottle, and coughed, then guzzled again. The fire grew in his belly. Oblivion would soon encroach, and that put a smile on his face—the promise of limitless freedom.

This was his futon, he knew, when he woke up, although he wasn't sure how he got here. Sunlight streamed in the windows. When he sat up, his head pounded and made him wince. Clothes were strewn on the floor. They all looked familiar. He must have gone to bed alone.

Rising, the pain was worse, and his heart started to pound. He had to sit down again on the bed as the nausea welled up, and he struggled not to let it overwhelm him, breathing deeply. Closing his eyes didn't help, as that made the room spin. Eventually he was able to stand, and went to the bathroom, splashing water on his face. He shook some ibuprofen tablets out of the little bottle into his mouth, then cupped his hands under the tap to get a mouthful of water.

The only thing in the Frigidaire was a jar of gherkins. The tart brine smelled tolerable when he cracked it open, so he fished a couple out and chewed them up, then climbed back into bed and dozed for a while.

When he woke again, it was late morning. He texted Max:

Are you in the office?

His reply buzzed Slater's phone a moment later:

I'll be in this afternoon.

That gave him time to sober up, and for the painkillers to kick in. As he sat up, he smelled an armpit. He definitely needed a shower. The hot water made him more alert, and he went to the kitchen and pulled the jar of powdered coffee out of the pantry cupboard. The bourbon bottle, sitting beside it on the shelf, had a startling volume missing from it. No wonder his head hurt. When he opened the coffee jar, there were just a few brown crumbs in the bottom, so he ditched it in the trash.

After he got dressed, he trotted down the two flights to his garage and drove downtown, turning onto Broadway, where he parked in a loading zone in front of the vegan doughnut shop and put on his flashers. Inside he waved over a clerk and pointed out a doughnut in the display case.

"A black coffee too," he said, pulling out his wad of cash as she tucked the greasy torus into a little box.

"We don't sell drinks."

"What the hell kind of doughnut joint doesn't have java?" he said irritably, watching her make change.

"There's a coffeehouse at the end of the block," she said, raising her eyebrows, "although I know it's a hardship to walk that far."

Taking his change and scooping up the box, he went out to the Thunderbird. It actually was a hardship—if he left his car here any longer, he'd get a fat parking ticket.

On the short drive to his office, he ate the doughnut, cradling the box in his lap. In the parking lot he waved to the attendant and headed across the street. As long as he bought a parking pass every month, those guys rarely asked to see it, as they knew his distinctive vehicle.

There were still some day laborers hanging around the entrance, waiting for gigs sewing or cutting fabric or hauling merchandise, and he stepped past them on his way in. When he got upstairs, Max was behind his desk, wearing his gray suit again today with a somber red necktie. Slater dropped into the chair across from him.

"You look like hell," Max said.

"Thank you." Slater ran a hand through his hair. "So you're starting on your window-shade case."

"Correct—the cheater is booked into that stupid hotel with all the cabanas. I'm spending the night in the one next door to his."

"That sounds expensive."

Max gestured vaguely. "It is, but it's the client's money. I have a source who works at the hotel. He's helping me out with surveillance."

"Steal me a bathrobe."

Max laughed at that. Those jobs were emotionally grisly, and Slater avoided them, but Max seemed to relish catching unfaithful spouses. Usually the clients were rich people who had lots to protect in their prenups and divorce settlements.

"I've been thinking about Jordan's story," Slater said. "The whole thing doesn't quite add up."

"He's a sweet guy, but he's crooked. I doubt anything he told us is true."

"That's why I want to look into the doctor who hired him."

"I won't dissuade you," Max said. "Anything that would help Jordan might improve my personal life."

"I know you're busy. I don't have anything on right now."

There was a knock at the door, and Max rose and stepped around his desk.

"Speaking of my personal life, that's Vanessa."

Slater waited for them to connect before he got up. He heard them embrace, and then Vanessa spoke.

"What's that?"

"His name is Rey," Max said. "He's bringing us good luck."

"He's very cute, but he needs to eat more carbs."

Slater stepped into the front office and greeted her. Around thirty, maybe, Vanessa wore her hair in myriad little braids and always looked polished. Today she was dressed in a print blouse and dark trousers.

"I'm glad I ran into you," she said. "Thanks for helping track down Jordan. I should have thought he might go to Willy in Bardo."

"He seems like a decent guy," Slater said.

"I just can't understand how he went off the rails."

"Slater might look into that doctor," Max said.

Her eyebrows shot up. "Why?"

"I got the sense that maybe Jordan got duped by this guy."

"That's Jordan's version. I'm not sure what to believe. They found a gun in his car." She sighed. "Max said you thought we should get him a lawyer. I made some calls this morning. At least he'll get decent advice now."

"That's the right thing to do," Slater said, "regardless of what the truth is."

"Let me get my jacket," Max said, and stepped into his office.

Vanessa gestured to the statue of Rey Pascual. "I like your new reaper mascot."

"I'm not sure if he's staying or not."

"Why is he wearing a crown?"

"I guess he's the king of something. *Rey* means king."

"It might work here. The skeleton motif feels a little dark, but I guess that's the nature of your business."

Max came back, adjusting his lapels. "We can't all decorate our offices with Fabergé eggs and Degas sculptures."

Vanessa frowned and shook her head, eyeing Slater. "I don't have any of those."

"Still, you wouldn't believe how much money they have over there," Max said. "They put gold leaf on everything. It looks like King Midas has been through."

"I know Cal Tech has a hefty endowment," Slater said.

"He's lying," she said, and laughed. "My office isn't much bigger than this one."

"It's a lot fancier, though," Max said.

"He means that I can see a tree from my office window," Vanessa said, looping her arm through

Max's. "I'll bring him back after lunch."

"Keep him as long as you want," Slater said. "Rent's not due for a while."

In his own office, it looked like there had been a blizzard, with paper everywhere. He'd forgotten about that. Slater spent a minute picking up all the printouts they'd made in the hunt for Jordan, and piled them in the wastebasket. Next he sat down, and swung his boots onto his desk, and pulled his computer keyboard into his lap. That greasy doughnut had helped a lot to take the edge off his queasiness, but after the exertion of cleaning up he felt a little shaky. He closed his eyes and took a few breaths before he set to work.

The first results that came up in a search for Thiago Sobel were about his medical practice, and clicking around, eventually Slater found a portrait of him, wearing a white lab coat, arms folded, beaming at the camera. As Jordan had said, Thiago was dark and Latin, and had a sharp money haircut. The creases around his eyes put him in his forties. The guy was basically fuckable, he decided.

The accompanying bio read like it had been prepared by a publicist, in snappy language that lauded his studies and prosaic career as if they were exceptional achievements. The text implied that Thiago saw regular patients, but mostly it talked about his work in cosmetic surgery.

Under the heading "Philanthropy" was a paragraph about an organization called Wart Zero. It was a nonprofit set up by Thiago to do dermatological work in impoverished parts of the Amazon basin. That sounded totally bogus—rich people sometimes set up charities that benefited only themselves, and this one was more than likely a tax dodge. A photo showed Thiago in safari drag, kneeling in front of lush tropical foliage to examine the shoulder of a half-naked toddler.

Slater opened another tab and found a charity watchdog site. It listed Wart Zero's rating as "Undetermined—inadequate information," explaining that it was difficult to verify the group's expenditures or achievements because the purported beneficiaries were in remote parts of Peru and Bolivia.

When he clicked through to Wart Zero's website, there were more photos of Thiago and others doing medical work, presumably burning warts off the indigenous denizens of the rainforest. In the top corner, a headline caught his eye: "Tickets still available." Slater read the details. It was a fund-raising event for the organization, happening tonight, and not far from here, in the ballroom of a downtown hotel. Thiago was named as the host—he'd definitely be there.

After he locked his computer, he set the keyboard on his desk and got up, and took a deep breath to steady himself. He flicked off the lights and paused to bolt the door as he left. Downstairs, he crossed the street to the parking lot, trotting to avoid an oncoming car, and climbed into the Thunderbird to drive the few blocks to the Financial District. At the office tower where Cudahy Mutual Insurance had its offices, he turned down the ramp into the garage.

His handler at the company, Della, regularly hired him to investigate insurance claims that made the bean counters nervous. As a contractor he could do things the company could never get away with, the dirty work that would otherwise sully the hands of the white-collar crowd. Of course, if anything he did blew up into a scandal, they could cut him loose and deny any responsibility. He hadn't heard from Della in a while, but maybe she could do some work for him.

The valet took his keys, and he went in and rode up to the thirty-fourth floor. As he stepped off the elevator, Della's receptionist, Crystal, looked up. Her face hardened into a scowl at the sight of him. Along with the plush lounge furniture and her broad beech-paneled desk, Crystal looked good out front—a requirement in an industry with lots of straight guys—in a sharp crimson suit, blood-red nails, her blond hair swept up. But she was no fan of Slater.

He stopped in front of her desk and raised his

eyebrows. "Is she in?"

"I'll check," she said, and reached for the phone.

Slater folded his arms and glared at her. She knew damn well whether Della was here or not.

"One of your grubby freelancers is here," Crystal said into the receiver. "It looks like he's been through the wringer. … I'll check." She looked up at him and raised her eyebrows. "What's your name?"

"Fuck you, you peroxide fascist," Slater growled, and strode toward the hallway that led to Della's office. That bougie desk jockey was well aware of his name.

Della's door was ajar, and when he pushed it open, she leaned back in her chair and beamed at him. Pushing sixty, she kept her hair sprayed into a cloud around her head, and today wore a gray plaid suit that accentuated her trim figure.

"And there he is," she said. "You really do look haggard."

"I've been working," Slater said, and dropped into the chair in front of her desk.

"In the middle of the freeway? You look like you've been run over by a truck."

"Vegas," he said, and gestured helplessly.

Della nodded. "You know, you should be nicer to Crystal. She could trip you up one day."

"Unless she's packing a heater, she's not going

to be slowing me down. Plus you don't pay me to be nice."

"True." She watched him for a moment. "I'm sorry there hasn't been a lot of work lately."

"I'm not worried. I made a little on that case with the stolen cars."

"That wasn't ours," she said, raising an eyebrow, "but I know exactly how much the reward was. You made out like a bandit."

Slater spread his palms. He couldn't argue with her assessment. A few days' work had netted him thirty grand.

"So—to what do I owe the pleasure?"

"Are you free this evening? I need a date."

Della recoiled visibly. "Did all my leering and innuendo finally sink in?"

"Not that kind of date. I'm going to a fundraiser, and I need arm candy."

"Stop it," she said, sitting up, her eyes bright.

"I'm serious. You always look money, and you fit in with that crowd. Rich folks, I mean."

"Who told you that I love to be flattered?"

"I also need someone who can get me close to the host. I know you know how to be nice."

"So you're on a job."

"In no way does that detract from your skills and charm."

"I'm not worried about that at all," she said. "I'll take what I can get. Show me the invite."

"It's on a website," Slater said, and recited it for her.

Della clacked at her keyboard and then peered at her screen. "Wart Zero. Never heard of it."

"Do you see the name of the host?"

Della clicked around, her brow furrowing. "Hosted by Dr. Thiago Sobel."

"That's the guy I want to talk to."

"If that's a recent photo, he's seriously dreamy. And Latin—just the way I like 'em." She shot Slater a pointed look before turning back to the screen. "It's black tie. You'll need a tux, and I'll need a gown. ... The program is at seven, with cocktails after. Unless you want to sit through a bunch of boring speeches, we should show up around eight."

"I knew it."

Della looked up at him, her eyes narrowing. "Knew what?"

"I knew you were the woman for the job. One glance and you already know how to maneuver through this stuff."

"Boring events like this are second nature." She sighed. "It sounds kind of sad when I say it out loud."

"So you're in?"

"Of course. Fund-raisers are mindless if you're there for the speeches. Going in undercover will be a blast."

"Excellent. What's your rate for an evening's work?"

She scowled at him. "I'm not going to take money from you for going to a party."

"That's your call," he said, and stood up. "I'd better buy the tickets."

"The hotel is two blocks from here. Meet me here at eight and we'll walk over." Della glanced at her watch. "That's less than six hours. I need to get a move on."

"Are you going to have to buy a dress?"

"I have one that'll work. The time crunch is about hair and makeup."

Walking back to the front office, Slater had to grin. Della was clearly excited about doing this. On his way past the reception desk, he noticed Crystal's smoldering glare.

"See you next Tuesday," he called to her, raising his arm in a brief wave.

When the valet brought his car, he climbed in and closed his eyes for a minute, taking deep breaths. He wasn't nauseous anymore, just seriously fatigued. From now on he was going to stick to the booze rules. Digging in the glove compartment, he found a bottle of aspirin, and shook some into his mouth, then ground them up between his teeth.

Slater had a tux, but not the shoes to go with it, or a belt that would fit. There was a vegan shoe store in the Arts District, not far away on the other side of downtown, and he drove there, pulling into a street space out front. After he explained what his tux looked like, the clerk sold him a belt and a pair of shiny black oxfords that would work. Back on the street, he put the bag with his purchases on the passenger's seat and drove to his apartment.

Upstairs, he threw the shoes on the sofa before he got undressed and climbed into bed, managing to set an alarm before the exhaustion overwhelmed him.

———

Later, waking to his bleeping phone, he felt a little better. He pulled the garment bag with his tux in it from the bedroom closet and got dressed. It was dark blue and cut trim, and it still seemed to fit. When he came to the bow tie, he draped it around his neck, then went out his front door and knocked on the one adjacent to it. His neighbor, Grace, was old-school—she would know how to tie a bow tie.

But Grace didn't answer, and there was no sound from within. Max had helped him with it last time, but he was too far away, stalking cheaters in Beverly Hills tonight. Back in his own apartment, he texted Andy:

Do you know how to tie a bow tie?

His reply came a moment later:

You're on your own, brother.

He sent the same query to Della, who texted him back, in all caps, an enthusiastic "yes" with a throbbing heart emoji.

Locking his front door, he trotted down the stairs to his garage. The new shoes felt thin and light and weird, almost like he was barefoot, but at least that made them easy to walk in.

The garage under Della's building was open, but it was after business hours, so there was no valet on duty, and plenty of open spots. He parked near the entrance and went up to Della's office. Crystal's desk was vacant, and so was Della's, although her door was open. Slater went inside and stepped over to the windows to admire the view of the city, glittering beneath the fading gray of twilight. He'd never been here at this time of day, when the lights were on. This town definitely looked better in the dark.

Della greeted him from the doorway, and when he turned around, he had to pause to take in the transformation. Her hair was dramatically styled and brushed back, and her makeup was heavier. The dress was off the shoulders, glamorous and cut low, made of an iridescent midnight-blue fabric.

"I love the tux," she said, looking him over.

Raising her voice an octave, she added, "We match."

"You look stunning," Slater said. "I feel like I could fall into your cleavage."

"That's the point," she said, raising an eyebrow. "These are amazing breasts. I know that to be an objective fact. They don't do anything for you?"

"It's like wandering around LACMA and looking at the art. I can appreciate it, but that doesn't mean I want to fuck it."

"That's what I like about you, Slater. You're subtle and eloquent."

"You said you know how to tie a bow tie."

"Sit down," she said, gesturing to the chair in front of her desk.

Della stood behind him and reached around his neck, leaning into his shoulders.

"You smell amazing," she said.

"I'm not wearing anything. It's just sweat."

"That's what I'm talking about." She tapped under his chin, and he tilted his head back to make room for her to work. "So you wouldn't even consider sleeping with a woman?"

"Not unless she was actually a man."

"That makes you sound like a chauvinist."

"I think I do a lot less damage to women because I'm not chasing them."

"Stand up," she said, and he faced her as she performed a final adjustment on the bow, frowning in concentration. "I think that does it. Do you want to have a look in the restroom mirror?"

"I'm sure it's fine."

"We can go, then."

Della grabbed a little silver clutch from her desk and closed her office door before they walked to the elevator. Once they were downstairs in the lobby, she stepped close to Slater and put her hand under his elbow, resting her palm on his forearm. The only other person who had ever done that was Doris, when she needed him to be strong, usually at funerals. He had to concentrate for a minute to adjust his stride to align with Della's.

They strode into the hotel and past the reception desk, into a long broad corridor lined with event rooms. It was easy to spot the Wart Zero function—it was the only room where the doors were open. A reception table was set up just outside, and several people were standing around, all of them in evening dress. From within the ballroom came the booming sound of a woman's voice amplified by a sound system.

As Slater stepped up to the table, the woman sitting behind it looked up at him expectantly.

"John Slade," he said.

She nodded and dug through a metal cash box, then pulled out two tickets, handing them to Slater.

As he stepped back, Della asked him quietly, "Is that one of your aliases?"

"I wasn't about to give these grifters my real name." He handed her one of the tickets.

Della didn't take it, instead meeting his eye. "The gentleman handles things like tickets."

"My god, woman—who's being the chauvinist now?"

 NINE

When they went inside, Slater handed over both tickets, and they stood near the entrance to take in the scene. One side of the room was filled with rows of chairs facing a low stage, where the speaker was standing and droning into a handheld mike. She wore a formal dark dress, and jewelry sparkled in the spotlight at her ears, on her fingers, around her neck.

Half the seats were occupied, and other people stood behind them on the open floor, and around the bar in the corner. Slater surveyed the crowd. Unlike what he saw in the real world, most of these people were white. There was a lot of gray hair among the tuxedo-clad men, and many of the women's faces had that idiosyncratic look of moneyed aging—dimpled by surgery, plumped with collagen, frozen by botox.

"If she had any more diamonds on, she'd qualify as her own cartel," Della said, gazing at the speaker.

"We underestimated how long the yapping would take," Slater said.

"I bet she's almost finished. People look restless."

She was right, as a moment later the speaker waved a glittering hand and said, "That's enough from me. Enjoy the evening."

The crowd applauded in relief, and many rose and drifted into the open space.

"I see the bar," Slater said, "but where's the food?"

"Maybe there isn't any."

"Who calls a party for seven o'clock and doesn't have hors d'oeuvres, at least?"

Della frowned. "It's not that odd, is it?"

"It's the most goyishe thing I've ever seen. Thiago is a Jew, and Jews put out food."

"How do you know he's Jewish?"

"It's an assumption. His surname is Jewish."

Della gestured to a waiter who appeared, moving through the crowd with a tray. "There's your snacks. They waited until after the speeches."

She stopped the waiter and took one of the dainty canapés.

"What are those?" Slater asked him.

"These are shrimp, and that's chicken."

"Send the vegan tray over this way."

"I don't think we have any of those," he said.

"Are you kidding me?" Slater demanded, raising his voice.

"Sorry," he said, eyeing Slater nervously as he stepped away.

"Let's not get eighty-sixed before you even see your target," Della said, and nibbled at her snack.

"For the price of those damn tickets, I expected to get fed. Maybe there's a vending machine for me in the servants' quarters."

"Seriously, though," Della said. "Who has an event in LA with meat-only canapés? It's not 1957."

Over her shoulder, Slater spotted Thiago. Dressed like everyone else, in a black evening suit, he stood near the stage, chatting with a small group of people, including the bling-laden woman who'd been on stage. His portrait hadn't shown how lithe he was—his close-fitting tux revealed the body of a runner. He looked to be at ease in the conversation, punctuating his words with animated gestures.

"That's the guy," Slater said.

Della subtly shifted position to take a look. "I recognize him from the invite. Nice butt."

"He's popular."

"The host never gets any downtime," she said, and dusted the crumbs off her fingers, then squared her shoulders. "Time for me to go to work."

From a distance Slater watched as she approached the throng surrounding Thiago, at first engaging a gray-haired man on the periphery. She flashed a smile, and tilted her head back to laugh at whatever he'd said, and touched him on the arm. Through him she drew a woman into the discussion, and then moved on to another. Her social skills were exquisitely fluid, and the men, especially, quickly succumbed to her charm. It was like watching a lioness pick off unsuspecting gazelles.

Within a few minutes she was standing next to Thiago. Slater moved in, using his elbows rather than charm to get close to them. Della was saying something about Bolivia, but when Thiago glanced at Slater, she instantly shifted gears.

"This is my friend Slater," Della said, taking a step toward him, deftly pulling him in.

Slater should have told her not to use his real name, but it was too late now. Thiago eyed him and said something in Spanish.

"I know I look Latin, but I don't actually speak the language," Slater said.

A hint of a smile played on his lips. "I get that

all the time too. I'm from Argentina, so people assume I'm Catholic."

"Sobel is a Jewish name, correct?" Della said.

Thiago nodded. "You're very insightful."

"I thought Argentina was where the Nazis went," Slater said. "Not the Jews."

"It's a pretty big place. There's room for both."

Slater could feel the weight of his gaze, the subtle challenge. It changed things—the guy was interested in him.

"Your suit is very chic," Thiago said. "Would you call the color sapphire?"

"I'd call it blue."

A man stepped in beside Della to speak to Thiago, pulling his attention away. Slater followed Della's lead when she turned to one of the other guests, and listened to her make small talk, her banter eliciting laughter as she gradually collected a small circle of her own. His instincts about her had been right—she was really good at this.

When there was a break in the conversation, Della pulled him aside.

"Do you want me to corner Thiago again?" she said.

"He can't keep his eyes off me. That puts the pursuit in my wheelhouse."

"Really," she said emphatically, and glanced over at Thiago. He had his hands in his pockets, listening earnestly to one of his guests. "I didn't pick up on that, but it makes sense—he didn't even glance at my boobs."

"I guess it's hard to tell sometimes."

"Well, if you've got it from here, I might bug out."

"You're a genius in this environment," Slater said. "You should be a diplomat."

"You're welcome," she said, but didn't move to leave.

"OK, then," Slater said, and waved his arm. "Bye."

Della scoffed. "Were you going to walk me to the taxi stand?"

"Right—that's exactly what I was thinking I should do." He held out his elbow, and walked with her into the hallway and toward the lobby.

"Those people loved you," Slater said. "I only heard some of it. What were you telling them?"

"The truth, partly, about working in insurance. I also expressed my deep concern about the impact of warts in the Amazon region."

Slater chuckled. "I bet that went over well."

"They all know it's a sham. People come to these things to network and get their names in the program."

A couple of taxis were waiting at the curb, and Slater pulled open the door of the one in front. Della kissed him on the cheek, a startling momentary swirl of proximity to her hair and makeup and perfume, then climbed in and waved as the car pulled away.

The party was thinning out, he saw, when he stepped back inside. As he crossed the ballroom toward the bar, he caught sight of Thiago, and met his intent gaze. Even though the guy was leaning in to talk to someone, as he was running his mouth, his eyes followed Slater. Looking away, he smiled to himself. Thiago was into him—he could let him do the work.

The crowd at the bar was gone, and he stepped up and ordered a soda water. This was still work, so according to his booze rules, he couldn't really drink.

Filling a highball glass with ice, the bartender said, "Just the water?"

"You could dump some vodka in it," he said, and looked over the crowd.

Slater was halfway through the glass, standing alone near the bar, when Thiago approached him.

"Your date abandoned you," Thiago said, his brow furrowing in mock concern.

"It wasn't that kind of date."

"She seems like a lovely lady." He flashed Slater a smile, dazzling and warm and inviting. This was a guy who knew how to leverage his looks—that smile could mesmerize the coldest cynic from a block away.

"I heard someone say that you're a doctor."

Thiago slid his hands into his pockets and puffed out his chest, a cocky smirk on his lips. "That is correct."

"Are you a surgeon?"

"No, but I work with surgeons. I'm a specialist."

Slater nodded. "I guess that's not as bad. Doctors are usually idiots, but surgeons are always assholes."

"That's a sweeping generalization," Thiago said, his face clouding. "It's also a little judgmental."

Slater waved a palm. "Nothing personal. Doctors are like those people who memorize twenty thousand digits of pi. You seem pretty functional, though, hosting an event like this."

"That almost sounded like a compliment," Thiago said, frowning. "Almost. And here I was thinking how charming you looked."

"You're conflating looks with behavior. 'Charming' is about pretty words and pleasant manners. Nobody ever called me that." He swirled the ice in his glass and held Thiago's eye. "But if you like the way my tux fits, that's a whole other discussion."

"So now you're flirting with me?"

"Hitting on you," Slater said. "Same idea, but with a lot less bullshit."

"I'm not sure if I should take you seriously

now. You just insulted me, and insulted my profession."

"I'm dead serious. You're hot. I'll fuck you, Doc, if that's what you want."

His eyes narrowed. "I admit that I'm tempted. Why am I so attracted to you when you're talking like a hood?"

"Pheromones, maybe? You'd have to ask a scientist."

Thiago took a deep breath and lowered his voice. "I have a room upstairs. Would you like to meet me there in half an hour or so, after I wind things up here?"

"Have you got a pen?"

Reaching inside his jacket, Thiago produced a black Sharpie. Slater took it and pulled the cap off, then handed it back to him and held out his palm.

Thiago blushed but took hold of Slater's hand, and quickly scrawled the room number on his skin. Not looking at Slater again, he tucked the pen away and smiled at a woman who was approaching them, then stepped away to greet her.

The delay gave Slater time to find dinner. He hadn't eaten earlier, and now his stomach was grumbling. Out in the hallway, walking toward the front of the hotel and the street outside, he checked on his phone for a decent *lonchera*, and found there was one parked a few blocks away.

Walking up to the truck, it wasn't too busy, and they'd thoughtfully put a bench on the sidewalk for their patrons. Slater ordered three jackfruit tacos and paid the woman, then waited by the rear window. Once he had them in hand, he sat on the bench and ate leaning forward, knees spread, so that he wouldn't drip hot sauce on his suit.

Two college-age women, both in short skirts and heels, collected their orders from the truck window and joined him on the bench. One of them had lavender hair, and the darker one had hers moussed up into a Trojan mane. They were obviously inebriated, laughing and talking loud.

"I love this town," the one sitting next to him said. "Here's a guy in a tux eating tacos from a food truck."

"Am I overdressed?" Slater said, eyeing her sidelong.

"No, man—look at us. It's party night."

"We're going to a new place. It'll be lit," the other one said, leaning past her friend to shoot him a look.

"On Monday night?"

"Totally. You should come with us."

"I can't. I've got a thing." Slater rose and tossed his wrappers in the trash barrel.

"What could be more important than party night?" she demanded.

"Work," Slater said, and jabbed his thumb

toward the hotel. "I have to go fuck a guy."

Walking away, he could hear the pair of them laughing.

In the middle of the block ahead he saw two pedestrians, a man and a woman, veer into the street and walk around a couple of parked cars before stepping up onto the sidewalk again. As he got closer, he could see what they were avoiding—a homeless guy, standing beside a parking meter at the curb, wearing a sleeping bag like a cape. There were no laces in his grimy tennis shoes, but he was suspiciously clean-shaven. Talking to himself, he waved his arms to emphasize his words.

"She's a pedophile," he muttered. "A goddamn pedophile. Pizza bus. Exo-licious. Con-marketed."

It was the babbling of an untreated schizophrenic, and Slater ignored him as he walked by.

"Wetback in a blue suit."

Slater stopped and turned back to him. "Are you talking to me?"

"You're the only wetback I see. You should wear brown, not blue."

Stepping closer, before the guy could react, Slater punched him on the chin, snapping his head. The guy stumbled backward, flattening himself against the parked car.

"Why did you do that?" he demanded, pulling

his sleeping bag tighter around him. "You can't just knock people out."

"If I wanted to knock you out, I would have coldcocked you, and you'd be out."

"He punched me," he shouted, looking around at the street, but there was no one else within earshot.

"That wasn't really a punch," Slater said. "It was a wake-up tap. I'm not one of the voices in your head—there are consequences for spouting your racist crap."

"Wetback," the guy spat.

Lightning fast, Slater struck him again, harder this time. The guy spun sideways, his ersatz cape twisting with him. Slater tried to stomp on his calf, which would have laid him out flat, but he couldn't locate it under the filthy matted fabric, and his foot struck the concrete instead, jerking the sleeping bag off his shoulder. The thin oxfords weren't built for this, and the ammonia-and-vinegar stench of the guy was acrid at close range, so he stepped back.

"You're a pedophile," the guy shouted, pulling his cape around him and shuffling away.

Back in the hotel, Slater approached the clerk at the reception desk. "Where's the men's room?"

She gave him a subtle once-over. If he'd been dressed in his usual denim and boots, she would have assumed he was like the guy with the sleeping bag, a resident of the streets. But the tux must have passed muster.

"Around the corner," she said, and recited the code he'd need to unlock the door.

Standing at the mirror, he committed the room number Thiago had written on his palm to memory before he washed his hands of taco sauce and any filth that might have transferred from the mouthy homeless guy.

In the lobby he boarded the elevator, and a minute later rapped on Thiago's door. When he pulled it open, Thiago looked completely different. Instead of the tux, he was wearing a sheer paisley bathrobe that bore the sheen of silk. His hair was slicked back now, and he had a tumbler in hand, with a finger of amber liquid in it. He looked a lot more relaxed than he had downstairs.

"You really came," he said, and stepped back so that Slater could enter.

It wasn't a very big room. As he walked inside, Slater caught a whiff of his cologne. That was kind of gross, but he could hold his nose.

"Do you want a drink? I've got a bottle of scotch."

"Dutch courage?" Slater asked.

"Not at all. It's just to take the edge off. I've had a long day."

Slater stepped closer to him and undid the belt on his robe, then pushed it off his shoulders.

Thiago let it fall to the floor, shifting his drink from one hand to the other.

"You're lean," Slater said, running his hands over his naked arms. "I can see all the muscles."

Thiago reached for his hair, but before he could touch it, Slater grabbed his wrist to stop him, rattling the ice in the tumbler in his other hand, and held it tightly.

"What are you doing?" Thiago said, alarm in his eyes.

Slater chuckled and released his grip. "You called me a hood before. I'm playing to type."

"I don't like games," Thiago said, his expression clouding.

"Now I've upset you."

Slater took the tumbler from him and set it on the credenza, then reached for his hand and gently guided it to his own head. Thiago pushed his fingers into Slater's thick hair, then pulled him closer, meeting his mouth in a sloppy kiss that tasted of scotch. Pulling back, he grasped the ends of Slater's bow tie and undid the knot, then unbuttoned his shirt.

He was enjoying this part, Slater saw, taking his time, his breath heavy as he undressed him. Standing closer, he pushed his hands inside Slater's jacket, sliding it off, and then his shirt. He unbuckled Slater's belt, then pulled on both ends to press his raging woody into him.

Slater reached down and grabbed his cock, eliciting a sigh, then pushed him backward onto the bed. Eyes bright, Thiago watched as he dropped his trousers. Despite his protest about playing games, he didn't seem to mind being manhandled. Slater climbed on the bed and straddled him, running his hands over his chest, and felt his musculature and his ribs, then leaned down to meet his mouth.

When he shifted onto his side, Thiago said solemnly, "Are you going to fuck me?"

"Have you got a condom?"

Thiago got up and went to his briefcase, lying on the credenza, and pulled it open, then dug around inside. He tossed a foil square to Slater along with a little tube of lube.

Once he'd rolled it on, and Thiago was beside him again, Slater pulled him closer, one hand behind his neck, exploring his mouth with his tongue as he worked a finger inside him. Shifting position, he penetrated him, moving slowly when he saw Thiago's pained expression. Gradually he relaxed into it, and Slater built up a rhythm until he was pounding him. With his hand on Thiago's throat, he could feel his pulse, and smell his hair. Slamming into him, he came, his body shuddering. Thiago was so turned on that it only took a moment with Slater's hand on his cock, their mouths locked together, for him to come too, wincing and grunting and then collapsing on his back.

As he caught his breath, Slater shifted closer and wrapped an arm around his torso, notching his knees behind Thiago's.

When his panting subsided, Thiago spoke. "Do you want a little scotch?"

"Quiet," Slater mumbled.

———•———

Waking later, he found Thiago sitting up against the headboard, watching him.

"How long have I been out?"

"Not long." Thiago folded his arms. "I want to know why you don't respect me. Don't bother denying it."

Slater sighed, and rolled onto his back. It was so typical. Once a guy got what he wanted—the sex—it was time for all the bullshit—expectations, demands, the airing of grievances.

"Of course I don't respect you," Slater said. "Why would I? I don't know anything about you."

"That just doesn't happen to me. Most people have a basic degree of respect for my work, my education."

"I don't live in that world," Slater said. "Tell me about Jordan."

Thiago's eyebrows shot up. "Jordan?"

"Young guy, buff, lots of hair. You know who

I'm talking about. Don't bother denying it."

"You know him?"

"Not really. I know he got popped for armed robbery, and I know that involves you."

"Who are you?" he said, his brow furrowing.

"I'm an insurance investigator."

"Jordan was insured? For what?"

"He missed his arraignment. I'm looking into it."

"I didn't know that," Thiago said, still eyeing him. "So this is an interview. Do you bed down with everyone you need to debrief?"

"Only the beautiful ones," Slater said, and slid his hand inside his thigh.

Thiago scoffed and pushed his hand away. "Jordan was a patient. He had a couple of little keloids on his arm. I took them off, and he couldn't pay me, so we did a trade."

"What kind of trade?"

"He mentioned that he was going to Las Vegas for a few days. I told him that if he could pick up an antique for me, I'd call it square. The deal was just for him to pick up the statue. I didn't tell him to rob anyone."

"The statue belongs to you? Not to Paola Martín?"

"Of course it's mine."

"So why didn't she just hand it over?"

"I'm sure she would have, if I'd gone myself,"

Thiago said, gesturing vaguely. "But I wasn't there. Apparently Jordan decided to brandish a pistol, and the situation quickly deteriorated."

"If the statue is yours, why did she have it?"

"I bought it at an antiques shop in Vegas, and inadvertently left it at her place. I was staying with her."

"She's a friend?"

"An acquaintance."

"Where's the statue now?"

"I have no idea," he said, raising his eyebrows.

Slater watched him for a moment. "Jordan got popped in LA. Did the police take the statue?"

"How should I know? I certainly didn't get it. I never saw Jordan after he went to Vegas."

"That's not what he says."

Thiago scoffed. "He's obviously lying."

"Why would he lie about that?"

"Ask him. Maybe he wanted to sell the antique. I'm shocked that you'd believe a person who robbed a doctor's office instead of me. Either way, I never got the statue."

It was a blatant lie—if he wanted the statue enough to hire Jordan to retrieve it, he would have at least asked the police about it. Even the indignation contorting Thiago's face wasn't very convincing.

"I have to go," Slater said, and got up. He grabbed his shirt from the floor and pulled it on, then met Thiago's eye. "I want to see you again."

"For your investigation, or for personal reasons?"

"More sex. If you can handle my disrespectfulness."

"You said it was because you didn't know me. That's a hardscrabble worldview, but at least I understand where you're coming from. Even if you weren't born on the Mexican ranchos, your parents were, or your grandparents. The peasant mentality runs strong. Once you get to know me a little, of course you'll respect me."

Slater suppressed a grin as he stepped into his trousers. Thiago was making a lot of assumptions about him. He found a business card in his hip pocket and handed it over. Propped up against the headboard with a pillow behind his back, Thiago studied it as Slater stooped to tie his shoes.

"Cudahy Mutual," Thiago said. "I've never heard of it."

"I'm not surprised," he said, straightening up. "They don't cover your kind of work. Botched surgeries and medical malpractice, I mean."

"You know what?" Thiago said, anger flashing in his eyes. "You said surgeons were assholes, but it's you. You're the asshole."

Slater watched him for a moment, hands on his hips. This was a sharp turn from his conciliatory tone of a moment ago.

Thiago jabbed a finger at him. "You."

"I know," he said gently, and turned to walk toward the door.

"Fuck you," Thiago spat.

"We'll do that next time," Slater said, pausing in the doorway. "Give me a call."

It wasn't that late, and there were still people out on the streets as Slater walked the few blocks to Della's office to retrieve his car. When he got into his apartment, he peeled off the tux in the living room and draped it over one arm of the sofa so he'd remember to get it cleaned. It felt good to be out of those stupid featherweight shoes.

Clad only in his skivvies, he stretched out in the recliner and checked on Conrad's location. The dot on the map was gray, meaning his phone was switched off, but the reason was evident: the last hit had been a few hours ago at JFK airport. The idiot was on his way home.

Later, he woke, cold and uncomfortable. Pushing himself out of the chair, he went to the kitchen and measured out his half glass of bourbon, then slammed it, enjoying the brief moment of pleasure as it burned his throat. "That has to be enough," he muttered to himself. Savoring the warmth in his belly, he climbed into bed.

In the morning Slater lay there for a while, pondering the different stories he'd been told about the antique statue. Everybody lied all the time, so both versions were likely fiction. Jordan said Thiago didn't even know what the statue was, and Thiago seemed indifferent about not getting his hands on it. That was the part that made the least sense.

He forced himself out of bed and went to wash up, then put a mug of water in the microwave to make coffee. But there wasn't any left, he remembered, when he opened the cupboard, and he killed the machine, then went back to bed, settling into the warmth of the covers.

On his phone he read about the Buddha and about Guanyin. Both appeared in various forms in religious art, but the Buddha was usually depicted as male, and Guanyin was female. As Jordan had explained, Guanyin hadn't attained enlightenment the way the Buddha had, but she definitely had supernatural powers.

He'd read enough, he decided, and dialed Max.

When he picked up, Slater asked, "How was your cabana?"

"Luxurious, although I didn't spend much time in it. I was outside half the night lurking in the bougainvillea."

"Ouch—that stuff is unforgiving." Slater told him about interviewing the doctor.

"It sounds like he's quite the stuffed shirt."

"That's the vibe," Slater said. "Plus he's lying to me. Do you know who Jordan's girlfriend is?"

"Her name is Nia. I don't have a number, but I know she works at a pot shop on the boardwalk in Venice. Close to the Washington end. She's easy to spot—her hair is in long braids, and she wears weird colored contact lenses."

After he ended the call, Slater got up and shaved his face in the bathroom mirror. He was seeing Doris later, so he had no choice. One he was dressed, he tucked a change of clothes into his satchel and headed down to his garage. From the wall rack he took a shovel, and pruning shears, and some other gardening gear and loaded them into the trunk of the Thunderbird.

The trip to Venice went fast on the freeway, uncongested at this time of day. He parked in a paid lot next to the beach and walked to a coffee-house, where he bought a bagel and a soy latte. Sitting on a stool at the window, he ate the bagel, so dried out that he had to chew it methodically. It took a while, and he watched the pedestrians rambling past, and stared absently at the ocean across the sand. The marine layer had burned off already, and sunlight glittered on the waves.

Once he'd finished, he went outside with his coffee and headed up the boardwalk. All the T-shirt stores and tattoo parlors and skate shops were open, but on a weekday morning the foot traffic was tame compared to the crowds that descended on warm afternoons.

The skunky tang of weed hit his nostrils before he even saw the first pot shop. Following the green arrow plastered on the sidewalk sign, he stepped in through the propped-open doors. Here in the front there was no product on display, only big laminated photos of it. The real thing was kept behind a heavy security door. A uni-formed guard stood in front of it, his gut hanging over his belt. He looked Slater over with an indif-ferent gaze.

There was no need to ask for Nia—the woman sitting at the front counter fit the profile Max had described. Her hair was in long braids, and she wore a billowy bright-yellow top over her curvy figure. When she looked up at him, her eyes were weird and gray, a stark contrast to her rich mocha skin tone. No way could she believe that those contacts looked real.

She smiled at him and said, "I just need to see your ID before you go in."

"I'm not buying," Slater said. "I wanted to talk to you. I'm a friend of Jordan's."

She folded her arms and gave him the once-over. "You don't look like any friend of his."

"Do you know where he is?"

"I am not going to drop a dime on him," she said, her tone sharp.

"That's not why I'm here," Slater said. "I already know where he is. I saw him on Sunday."

"You're lying," she said, but there was uncertainty in her voice.

"I was with him when he left you that voice mail." He mimicked Jordan's soft tone. "Love you, baby girl.'"

Her eyes grew wide. "Where is he?"

Slater glanced briefly at the guard. "Do you have a break coming up?"

Nia sighed and picked up the desk phone, murmuring into it. A moment later a man came out of the back. He was about her age, with his head shaved smooth, and eyed Slater with interest as he stepped up behind the counter. Briefly acknowledging him, Nia moved past the guard and out toward the boardwalk, gesturing for Slater to follow.

"Do you want a coffee or something?" Slater said.

"No—let's go sit on the grass."

She led him toward the shore, across the bicycle path, and dropped onto a patch of greenery under a trio of washingtonias. Slater sat beside her, facing the ocean. Beyond the wide swath of sand he could hear the low rumble of the waves landing.

"I never come down here," he said. "It's like a different planet."

"So where is he?" Nia demanded.

"Back in jail in Vegas. He has to answer for a bench warrant."

"That dumb-ass. I told him not to skip out." She frowned at him. "Who are you, anyway?"

"I'm an investigator."

"Working for who?"

"The people who posted his bail. I'm trying to figure out why he did what he did. Has he been in trouble before?"

"He's a college boy, not a gangbanger," she said. "That's where we met. We graduated together a couple of years ago."

"So what happened?"

"Jordan doesn't deny what he did, but it's Thiago's fault. That oxy-pusher put him up to it."

"He's a drug dealer?"

She waved a hand. "It's just a figure of speech. I meant he's a doctor. Jordan is suggestible, and Thiago pressured him into doing the robbery. I can't believe Jordan is going away for that douchebag and his piece of garbage statue."

"Have you seen it?" Slater said.

"Jordan showed it to me when he got back to town. He didn't tell me the part about the gun until later."

"What did he do with the statue?"

She frowned. "He took it to Thiago, like he promised he would."

"When was that?"

"I saw Jordan the night he got back from Vegas. The next morning he delivered it to Thiago. He came down here after that, all happy to be done with it. Then he got busted. It was the same day."

"And he still had the weapon."

"Like I said, he's a dumb-ass sometimes."

"When Jordan got out on bail, he came back to LA?"

She sighed. "That's when he decided to skip out. He didn't tell me where he was going."

"When you're on the lam, it's smart not to advertise," Slater said, and stood up.

"Do you think you can get him out?"

He shook his head. "That's not going to happen. But he does have a lawyer working with him. That should minimize his sentence."

Nia looked out at the ocean. "Thiago is the real crook. I'd love to see that fucker nailed to the wall."

Walking back toward his car, Slater paused at the bike path to let a flock of spandex-clad speedsters whiz by. On his phone he checked Thiago's office hours. He'd be there now.

Once he was in the Thunderbird, he navigated to the 10 and headed toward Beverly Hills. Thiago's office was on a boulevard in a nondescript medical building, one of so many in this neighborhood. Medical providers thought that the Beverly Hills address gave them gravitas, but it was all about perception—there was nothing inherent about this zip code that elevated the quality of their work. To Slater it made them look bougie, a category that definitely described Thiago. The guy was condescending too, offhandedly calling him a peasant, and according to Nia, he was a manipulative lowlife. Slater needed to dig deeper into this guy. He probably shouldn't have slept with him.

He parked in the garage under the medical building and went upstairs to find Thiago's office. The waiting room was small, with half a dozen chairs lining the walls, devoid of patients. The only person in view was at the reception desk at the back—a chubby guy in burgundy nurse's scrubs. He was in his early twenties, maybe, and had mousy brown hair like Max's.

"I need to see Thiago," Slater said, approaching the desk.

The guy looked up and gave him a pointed once-over. "Dr. Sobel can't see walk-ins."

"That's a terrible customer-service attitude," Slater said, and moved past the desk, toward the hallway into the back.

The guy stood up and stepped in front of him, arching his back to emphasize his bulk, and held out his arm. "Are you deaf, cowboy?"

Even though he was a few inches taller than Slater, it was evident in the way he moved that he didn't really know how to impede someone's progress. Slater quickly slapped him, left and right, a firm kovac, then grabbed the front of his shirt and shoved him back against the wall.

The guy shouted in surprise, then made the classic amateur mistake of grabbing Slater's arm with both hands, struggling to get him to let go. That left Slater's other hand free to slap him again. The guy squeezed his eyes shut and tried to swat him away.

The first door in the hallway swung open, and Thiago appeared, wearing a white clinician's coat with his name embroidered in blue on the breast pocket. Slater cuffed the receptionist one last time and stepped back.

"What's going on?" Thiago demanded.

"I was teaching your henchman some manners."

"That's my receptionist."

"You can't push me around," the guy spat, massaging his cheek with his hand.

"I just did," Slater said. "It was actually pretty easy."

He took a step toward Slater, jutting his chin. It was only the empty posturing of a thwarted ego, but it was a mistake. Slater lunged for him, making a feint with his right hand. The receptionist flinched and held up his arms to block him, which left his other side exposed. Slater quickly slapped his face, then shoved his arm aside and backhanded him on the other cheek.

"Stop it," Thiago shouted. "What is wrong with you?"

Slater stepped back, warily eyeing the guy.

"I'm calling the police," he said, his voice breaking.

"Settle down, Arnold," Thiago said. "There's no need for that kind of distraction today." He glared at Slater and beckoned him into the inner office, then closed the door behind them. "What the hell was that?"

"Your lackey started it," Slater said. "He came at me."

To Slater's surprise, Thiago's demeanor softened, and he cracked a smile. "Your hands were moving so fast."

"It's called a kovac. It doesn't really hurt. It's used to get someone's attention."

"Is it from martial arts?"

"I don't think so. In Japan it's called *oufuku binta,* a round-trip slap. I've heard it called the paintbrush, and a cop I know called it the Joan Crawford. She used to do that in her movies."

"You have quite the knowledge base."

Slater stepped into the middle of the office and looked around. It was much larger than the waiting room, and had dark paneling and a huge Persian carpet that stretched almost to the walls. It made the place look like a cigar lounge. Thiago's desk was the size of a CEO's, with bookcases lining the wall behind it. There was no sign of a statue.

"I see what you're doing here," Slater said.

"What's that?"

"The wood paneling, and all the empty floor space. It projects wealth."

"How would you know? Somehow you got into my fund-raiser, but I'm pretty sure you're from the other end of the economy."

"My mother has some prosperous relatives,"

Slater said affably. "I've been in their houses. Like you, they're some of god's chosen people."

"You're Jewish?" Thiago said, raising an eyebrow. "I guess somebody's got to fill in the ends of the bell curve. What are the family names?"

"Her name was Moskowitz."

He nodded. "That's pretty hebe-y."

Slater put his hands on his hips. "It's a good thing you're Jewish. Otherwise I'd have to punch you in the face."

Thiago waved impatiently. "Enough with the violence. I have patients to see today. Why are you here? I told you everything I know about Jordan and his crime spree."

"It wasn't a spree—he took one thing from one place. It wouldn't even have been a crime if he hadn't flashed the weapon you gave him."

"I didn't give him a weapon. That's outrageous. Did he tell you that?"

"So it wasn't from you?"

"Of course not. Do I look like a gangster?"

Slater took a step toward him. "You did get a little rough when your clothes were off."

Thiago dropped his chin. "You're just saying that."

As he moved closer, Slater could see that he was breathing hard. Reaching inside his white coat, he felt along Thiago's belt, then leaned in to meet his taut warm mouth, exploring it, getting lost in it.

After a minute Thiago pulled back and laid a palm on Slater's chest. "I'm free later."

Slater grasped his belt and pressed against him so that Thiago could feel the woody that was tightening his jeans.

"Stop it," Thiago said, but he didn't pull away, instead nuzzling his neck, then ran his fingers into Slater's hair. Finally he stepped back and met his gaze. "I'll call you tonight."

On his way out, he saw that Arnold was sitting at his desk. One of the waiting-room chairs was occupied now, by a woman engrossed in her phone.

"Bye, Arnold," Slater said, and flashed him a smile, then double-clicked his tongue.

The traffic on La Cienega was sluggish on the way back to the freeway. On the seat beside him, his phone sounded with a familiar ring tone: *"No wire hangers ... ever! I buy you three-hundred-dollar dresses, and you treat them like they were some dishrag!"* Slater took a breath to steel himself before he picked up.

"What do you need, Doris?"

"I don't need a reason to speak to my son. I wondered if we were still on for today."

He sighed audibly. "I'm on my way there now."

"Lovely. I'll make us lunch."

Doris's place was in hilly Mount Washington, and he exited the freeway, navigating up into her neighborhood. She'd acquired the modest house as a single parent on a teacher's salary, but she'd paid off the mortgage, and it was worth a lot more now than when she'd bought it. Slater wanted her to sell it and move up the coast somewhere like a normal retired person. He'd even picked out a town that was far enough away from LA for his comfort. But so far there had been no talk of movement.

Doris's Buick was the only car in the driveway, and he pulled in behind it. Thankfully her idiot boyfriend Albert's midlife-crisis Boxster was nowhere to be seen.

Opening the trunk of the Thunderbird, he pulled on his work gloves, then took the shovel and the pruning shears and walked around to the backyard. First he deadheaded the rosebushes and cut back the canes. They were still blooming riotously in reds and whites and pinks, perfuming the yard with their sweet scent. Next he pruned the wisteria and rearranged some of its twisting vines. Its glorious cascading flowers peaked in May, so it was done for the year.

In the garden shed he found a bag of dry horse manure and carried it over to the bed where Doris had planted artichokes. Kneeling in the dirt, he dug into the soil with his gloved hands. It was loose enough that he didn't need a trowel. Scooping out a few handfuls of fertilizer, he started massaging it in around the roots with his fingers.

The back door to the house swung open, and Doris stepped outside, beaming at him. Petite and wearing black pants and a blue fitted shirt, these days she was letting some gray show in her dark hair.

"You're always so content when you're gardening."

Slater sat back on his heels. "It's nice to get my hands dirty once in a while. I can reconnect with the earth. Plus it gives me time to think."

"Listen to you," she said. "My philosophical son."

"Your seasonal son. There's lots of work to be done at the end of spring."

"One of the girls told me that I have the tightest rosebushes she's ever seen."

Slater laughed. "That's a good word for them."

He went back to work, and Doris stood there for a while to chat, filling him in on her social life. Eventually she went back inside. When he was almost finished, the back door swung open again, and Conrad stepped out, a big crooked smile on his face.

"It smells like a riding stable out here."

"What the fuck are you doing here?" Slater demanded.

"Don't be such a hothead," Conrad said. "I'm helping Doris." He was dressed for a day off, in denim and a summer shirt with birds of paradise printed on it. Barrel-chested even when he wasn't wearing a ballistic vest, Conrad had dark hair, and broad shoulders, and fit into his jeans in an achingly sublime way.

Doris stepped out behind him, and Slater threw up his hands.

"Why do you hang out with him?"

"You don't get to decide who I hang out with," she said.

"Yeah, well, make sure your jewelry is hidden."

Conrad chuckled. "Like I came here to steal."

Slater swirled a gloved hand at him. "All I see is a miasma of lies."

"You're the one who's up to your elbows in horse dirt," Doris said. "Literally and metaphorically. I asked Conrad over to help you move my sofa to the curb. Tomorrow is bulky trash pickup."

"What's wrong with your sofa?"

"It's a wreck. I'm getting a new one. I could have hired a couple of day laborers from the hardware store, but why would I do that when I have you two stalwarts?"

ELEVEN

oris went inside, and Slater went back to work.

"What were you doing in New York?"

"It was kind of a conference," Conrad said, and slid his hands in his pockets, and told him about it.

When he'd finished with the fertilizer, Slater brushed the dirt off his pants, and watered everything with the hose, then went around to his car at the front of the house. Conrad's familiar SUV was parked at the curb. It was a quiet street, so he didn't bother to go inside, and pulled off his boots and changed clothes there in the driveway. In the trunk of the Thunderbird he stuffed the dirty clothes and the gloves into a trash bag, then tied it tightly so that the car wouldn't smell like manure.

When he stepped in the front door, he saw that the dining table was set for three.

"Are you ready to eat?" Doris said.

"Let's do the manual labor first," Conrad said.

Doris propped the front door open, and Conrad picked up one end of the sofa as Slater lifted the other. It took a minute to maneuver it outside, with Conrad leading the way. They carried it past the cars to the bottom of the drive.

Watching Conrad work, and the perfect shape of his torso, Slater remembered the feeling of his skin, what his hair smelled like, the taste of his mouth. They dropped the sofa at the curb, and Conrad straightened up, arching his back, and flashed him that easy smile. Such a beautiful man. Slater could feel a lump in his throat as they walked back to the house. What an idiotic reaction that was. The guy had dumped him ages ago.

They both washed up, and the three of them sat at the dining table. Doris had made tomato soup and sandwiches. She told them of her adventures shopping for a new sofa, and asked Conrad about the event he'd been at in New York. Watching him talk, Slater saw how effortlessly he charmed Doris, and held her attention, and made her laugh.

"It was so sweaty there," Conrad said. "It's only June but it felt like a sauna." He eyed Slater. "Why were you in Vegas?"

Doris frowned over her sandwich. "You went to Vegas?"

"For about ten minutes. My partner collared a bail jumper, and we drove him up there."

After they'd eaten, Slater shifted his chair back. "I have to go."

Doris walked him to the front door. "Thanks for all your hard work."

Slater leaned down to kiss her. "Love you." Eyeing Conrad, he added, "Call me if he makes any trouble."

Before he backed out of the driveway, he texted Andy:

Can I drop by?

His reply came a moment later:

Sure. Done with work.

Traffic on the way downtown was sluggish with evening commuters. When he finally got to Broadway and parked, Andy greeted him at the door, barefoot, wearing boxer shorts and an orange T-shirt.

"Are you here to … use me for sex?" Andy said, waving him in.

"If you want. We could also just sit."

Andy knew what he meant, and broke into a smile. "I love doing that."

Slater followed him to the windows and

dropped into one of the easy chairs. Andy sat in his lap, leaning into him. Steadying him with an arm wrapped firmly around his waist, Slater relished the heat of his skin.

"How did we even invent this?" Andy said, his hands telegraphing his rhythmic muscle movements to Slater's shoulders.

"I think it was instinctive," Slater murmured.

Nuzzling his neck, he ran his hand under Andy's shirt, exploring his skin, pressing into his random twitches. He buried his nose in Andy's armpit, inhaling the fresh smell of his sweat, and tightened his arms around him.

"What's going on with you?" Andy said, ruffling his hair.

He loosened his grip. "What are you talking about?"

"You seem kind of blue."

"I don't do that."

"I forgot—you don't actually experience emotions."

Slater scoffed and massaged his neck. "I saw my ex today."

"Right—Doris said he was ... back from the East."

Pulling back, Slater glared at him. "And you wonder why I suspect the three of you are some kind of nefarious cabal."

"A cabal implies ... secrecy," Andy said,

smoothing Slater's hair. "It's no secret that I talk to your mother, and that your … ex does. That word also means people with … power. None of us have any power over you. Nobody tells Slater what to do."

"That's a good attitude," he said flatly. "Doris isn't trying to set you up with Conrad, is she?"

Andy laughed, the mirth rippling through his body. "She'd never do something like that."

"I'm not so sure."

"That guy isn't my type anyway."

Slater brushed the hair away from Andy's eyes. "No?"

"I go more for the … ratty and beat-up type. Scrapes and bruises. Not afraid to throw a punch."

"I see."

"The kind that you can't quite tell whether he's homeless or not."

"I get it," Slater said, and swatted his butt. "Knock it off."

Andy chuckled and leaned in to meet his mouth, hot and firm and intense.

Slater started to get hard, and Andy pulled away.

"I sense a … local uprising," Andy said. "I could rock your world, but I have to eat something first."

"Let's just do that, then. I have to work later."

"We'll go out."

Andy got up and went to his clothes closet to pull on a shirt and his cargo shorts. It took him a while, and the movement of his hands always looked random and disorganized to Slater, but from the chaos he made steady progress, and eventually he was dressed to go out.

"What are you waiting for?" Andy said, eyeing him as he slipped his arms into the cuffs of his walking sticks.

Slater had to grin at that, and followed him out into the hall.

The central market was just a couple of blocks away, and they strolled there at Andy's leisurely pace. In earlier times it had been an actual produce market, but the irresistible force of gentrification had turned it into a warren of pricey eateries. Instead of Latin matriarchs browsing the vegetable stands of yore, moneyed Anglo youths stood in line for trendy burgers and ramen.

They settled on the falafel place as it didn't have a line. It was set up like a bar, with stools lining a service counter, and they sat just off the busy aisle, where the crowds streamed past at Slater's elbow. The waiter, a lanky redheaded guy, took their order and brought them water, briefly flashing Slater a smile.

"Are you flirting with the redhead?" Andy demanded, once the guy had stepped away.

Slater scoffed. "He's flirting with me. I'm here with you. My focus is all about Andy." He put a hand on his back, then leaned in to kiss him on the neck.

"I know that's total jive. But it makes me feel good anyway."

When they were halfway through their meals, one of the many people walking past stopped and greeted Andy. He was twenty-something, and Latin, and had great hair. Suspiciously, he was blushing.

"It's good to see you," Andy said.

Slater folded his arms and glared at him, but the guy avoided his gaze.

"I just ate over there," he said, gesturing vaguely. "I can't believe what this place has become. My mom used to bring us here every Saturday to buy groceries."

"I never saw its … previous incarnation," Andy said.

"You live so close, and I'm down here all the time. You should call me."

"I will," Andy said, and turned back to his falafel when the guy walked away.

"Who the fuck was that?" Slater demanded.

"A friend from program."

"Bullshit. You slept with him."

"He's still a friend from program. And so what? You … do that."

Slater felt his heart pounding. There was nothing to say—it was true. The buzz in his pocket a minute ago was probably about the hookup he'd arranged for later. Still, it pissed him off.

The waiter stepped over and took his empty plate.

"It's always the … ego with boozers," Andy said. "You have no reason to be jealous."

"I'm not jealous," Slater growled. "Why are you fucking that twink?"

"Calm down," Andy said, raising his voice. "I'm here with you, not with him. Focus on that."

After Andy had finished eating, they walked back to his building. Twilight had descended, and the streetlights were coming on.

"You can come up, if you want," Andy said, pausing in front of his door and leaning on his sticks.

"I have to work," Slater said, and leaned in to kiss him. "Good night, beautiful."

Walking around to the parking lot where he'd left the Thunderbird, Slater checked his phone. Thiago had texted him:

Would you like to come to my house?

A subsequent message contained his street address. That simplified things—he wanted to have a look in Thiago's house, and now he didn't have to come up with an excuse, or explain that his own apartment was way too down-market for a fancy professional like him. Slater texted back:

On my way.

Driving out of the parking lot, he flicked on his headlights and headed toward West Hollywood. The address Thiago had given him was on a quiet side street of modest 1940s bungalows, where even the decrepit little fixers were worth over a million bucks. Thiago's had been renovated, by the look of the windows and the fence around the yard, and it was one of the few on the block that had a second story, so it was probably worth a lot more.

The gate to the driveway was open, so Slater pulled in and parked behind a Land Rover. It was quiet in suburbia, he realized—when he killed the engine and climbed out, he could hear the night insects, and the subtle *tick-tick-tick* of the Thunderbird's metal parts cooling off.

No cameras on the outside, Slater saw, at least not that he could see. The yard was landscaped with dryland plants, and a series of pavers, lined by Mexican feather grass, led to the entrance. When Slater rang the bell, Thiago pulled open the door, dressed in chinos and a polo shirt.

"What's with the feather grass?" Slater demanded.

"Is that what it's called? Do you like it? It's drought-tolerant."

"It's also an invasive. That stuff shouldn't be planted anywhere in California. It's like inviting the Red Army into your yard."

Thiago frowned. "It wasn't my decision. The landscaper did everything."

"Tell your gardener to cut them extremely short. They'll look OK but they won't reproduce and take over."

"Noted. So are you coming in?"

Slater stepped past him into the foyer and looked around while Thiago closed the door. Through an archway on the left was a dining room, its chandelier turned down low. A flight of stairs led up toward the back of the house, and on the right side was a half-open door to a dark room.

"You renovated the house?" Slater said. "The interior looks new."

"Not personally. I bought it and paid someone to update it. I've been here about a year."

"You don't feel out of place as a Latino in a super white neighborhood?"

"It's not that white."

"It is compared to my neighborhood."

"Where's that?"

"You've probably driven through it with your doors locked. It's called Westlake."

Thiago scoffed. "I may have heard of it. Why do you live down there? It feels like the Third World."

"It's where I need to be." Slater nodded to the dining table and the chandelier. "My whole apartment would fit inside that room. There's obviously good money in being a quack."

"You abrasive little *shvants*," Thiago said, anger flashing in his eyes. "Nobody talks to me that way. I'm starting to think you do it on purpose."

Slater turned to face him, and put his hands on his hips. "Maybe you need to be disrespected once in a while. Maybe it gives you some perspective."

Taking a deep breath, Thiago watched him for a moment. "I'm a sucker. It's that square jaw. You looked so hot in that tux—you were the only thing to look at in that whole ballroom. Like a museum with only one painting on the wall. And today, with those jeans."

"I suspect you're interested in more than my clothes." Slater stepped closer, cradling his head in his hands, and kissed him.

"Come upstairs," Thiago said softly.

"Don't I get the tour first?" Slater stepped back. "That's obviously the dining room, and the kitchen must be back there. What's in here?"

He stepped through the doorway at the foot of the stairs and groped for the light switch.

There was a desk facing the front window, he saw when the lights came up, with bookcases flanking it. Farther back was a dark leather-bound suite of chairs and a sofa.

"My office," Thiago said, stepping in behind him.

"You already have one in Beverly Hills. Do you really need two of them?"

The shelves mostly held books, with a TV set lower down, but the lone tchotchke is what caught his eye: a statue of Guanyin, maybe eighteen inches tall, in mottled blue-gray stone.

"Do you collect this stuff?" Slater said, gesturing to the statue. "That's the kind of thing Jordan jacked for you."

"That was a different piece," Thiago said. "The one I bought in Las Vegas had no archeological value. This one is quite expensive."

Slater took a step toward it.

"Please don't touch it," he said quickly. "It's very old. The oil from your hands will damage it."

Slater looked it over. "What do you call it?"

"It doesn't have a specific title, but it's a depiction of Buddha."

Jordan was right—Thiago didn't even know what he had. The feminine breasts, the folds of fabric draped over her hair—this was unmistakably Guanyin.

Slater turned to face him. "You said something

about going upstairs."

Thiago waited for him to step back into the foyer, then flicked off the lights and closed the office door. He led Slater up to the master bedroom, where the windows had a view toward downtown, the distant office towers visible above the treetops of the intermediate neighborhoods.

When he turned away from the window, Thiago had already pulled his shirt off.

"Slow down, Seabiscuit," Slater said. "Let me do that."

Standing close to him, pushing his hands aside, Slater unbuckled Thiago's belt, and zipped down his fly, then ran his hands slowly over his butt as he pushed down his chinos. Thiago was already hard.

"So what do you like to do?" Slater said, stepping back to admire his body.

"The stuff we did last time was fun."

"What part of it turned you on?"

"I liked the feeling of your hands on me," Thiago said. "The strength in them. You can be a little rough, if you want."

Slater nodded. "I know how to do that." He stepped closer and grabbed his throat.

Thiago instinctively pawed at his arm. People always did that, unless they'd been trained not to, and it made it easy for Slater to sweep his boot behind his calves and throw him off balance, onto the bed. Climbing on top of him, Slater slapped his face.

The blow hadn't been that hard, but Thiago said, "Whoa—dial it down a little."

"OK," Slater said, and unbuttoned his own shirt, and pulled it off, then leaned in to kiss him, pressing into Thiago's raging woody beneath him.

Thiago reached for Slater's belt, and unbuckled it, pulling his fly open. Slater got up to kick off his boots and ditch his jeans, then climbed up to straddle him again, relishing the heat of his skin. Thiago reached for his face, and Slater grabbed his wrist, and held fast. Thiago gasped, struggling with him, his eyes bright. This is what he wanted, Slater realized, and grabbed his other wrist, forcing his arms to his sides and then leaning in to mouth his neck and his chest.

"Condoms?" Slater said finally, releasing his grip.

Thiago shifted to the side of the bed and pulled a tray from beneath it. Once he'd unwrapped it and handed it over, Slater grabbed his throat again and pushed him onto his back, then rolled the condom onto Thiago. Straddling him, he lubed Thiago's cock and guided it inside him, then grabbed his forearms, and held him down, and sank onto him. Thiago's face contorted with the intensity of it, and he bucked and thrust until he came.

Slater stretched out beside him, and Thiago grabbed his cock.

"Do you want to fuck me?" he said quietly.

"Just do what you're doing," Slater said, and mouthed his jaw and his ear, burrowing his nose into his hair, and soon he climaxed.

Afterward, lying next to him, Thiago said softly, "You can stay if you want."

"I have to be up early."

"Are you still investigating Jordan?"

"I'm done with that guy. He skipped on his arraignment, so he won't be out again before his trial. After that he'll be eating baloney sandwiches in state prison for at least three years."

"That's unfortunate."

Slater sat up and found his shirt, then pulled on his jeans.

"Do you want me to walk you out?" Thiago said.

"I remember where the door is."

Slater trotted down the stairs and past the dimly lit dining room. He was tempted to duck into the office and take a closer look at that Guanyin statue, but he didn't, and closed the front door behind him as he stepped outside.

There was no need to look at the statue again—it was definitely the one Jordan had brought to him from Vegas. But Slater needed to get one more version of the story.

Driving back to his own apartment, he formulated a plan. Once the Thunderbird was safe in the garage, he went upstairs and stretched out on the recliner with his phone. The details for Paola Martín's medical practice in Las Vegas said that she had office hours tomorrow. Slater studied her portrait for a moment so that he'd recognize her. Next he found the number for the guy who brokered seats on little airplanes. It cost a lot more than flying from LAX, but there was way less hassle, and everything happened a lot faster.

"I need to go to Vegas in the morning," Slater told the voice mail, and gave his name. "I'll need two or three hours there on the ground before the return flight. I don't care what airport it leaves from."

In the kitchen he measured out his half tumbler of bourbon, then slammed it, relishing the burn. This was the best moment of the day, making everything else he did wan and colorless in comparison. The warm amber glow in his belly started to suffuse his body, slow his mind. After he peeled his clothes off, he set an alarm for early and crawled into bed to crash.

TWELVE

There was a message from the seat broker, he saw, grabbing his phone when its alarm woke him up.

You're leaving El Monte at 8 sharp. There's a return at 11:30. Transfer funds before flight time to confirm.

That gave him over an hour before he had to be there—plenty of time. Slater sent the money and then climbed out of bed and got dressed. Even in the morning traffic it didn't take long to drive to the dinky airport in El Monte, straight east on the 10. He parked in front of a row of buildings that looked more like retail outlets than aviation businesses, then locked the Thunderbird and walked into the broker's storefront.

There weren't any security procedures, and the clerk who greeted him sent him out the rear door onto the tarmac. He was the last of the six passengers to board the little jet, stooping to walk back to the only empty seat.

The woman sitting across from him looked over and murmured a greeting. She had her hair pulled back and rhinestone-studded sunglasses perched on her head. The gaudy jewelry at her ears and on her fingers said money, but incongruously her black track suit implied she was traveling incognito.

She held up a steel thermos and waggled it. "Martini?"

"Do you know what time it is?" Slater said.

"It's always martini time in Sin City. I made a whole bottle."

"I need to stay sharp."

"I love that you can bring your own booze on these little planes," she said.

"I love how quiet it is on these little planes."

She shot him a frown and turned away.

Soon they were in the air, and Slater watched the city fall away below. Then came the mountains, with the peak of San Gorgonio still dusted with snow, and after that, the vast Mojave crawling by. Settling back, he closed his eyes for a while. He really hated Vegas.

When they touched down, Slater turned on

his phone and ordered a ride-share. Walking out to the street through the little terminal, the other passengers seemed to be together, acting all boisterous, as if they'd each had one of those thermos martinis on the way. A mustard-yellow Humvee van was parked and idling at the curb, and the vacationers started climbing into it.

In front of the Humvee sat a black town car. The passenger window rolled down, and the driver called to him, "Slater?"

"I was expecting a Toyota," Slater said, climbing into the backseat.

"It'll be the same cost. I guess nobody needs a town car right now."

Twenty minutes later, the driver slowed in front of a strip mall, and turned into the parking lot. It was an odd venue for a medical office, but this was the right place—Paola's name was there on one of the storefronts, between a Thai take-out joint and a nail salon. The lot was almost empty, and it felt desolate, but maybe this was how things worked in suburban Vegas.

As he climbed out of the town car, he watched as a middle-age woman and a young man, maybe even a teenager, went into Paola's office through the storefront-style glass door. Slater followed them inside. The waiting room was lined with chairs, and reading lamps, and worn magazines strewn on a couple of end tables.

The place was devoid of life, apart from the pair he'd followed in. Then he spotted a little girl, sitting cross-legged on the floor in front of the reception counter. Clad in a tutu, she had a pink backpack zipped open beside her, and colored pencils and paper arrayed around. Not glancing up at the newcomers, she was studying the illustrations in a big picture book.

The young guy pulled out his phone and slouched in a chair, looking bored before he even glanced at the screen. Slater followed the woman to the counter, and a moment later Paola stepped out of the back, looking frazzled. The way Jordan had described Thiago correlated to Paola, but she was the European kind of Latin American. In her forties, maybe, she had wavy black hair bundled at her neck and wore a clinician's white coat.

"Marion," Paola said, greeting the woman, with no trace of an accent. "My receptionist called in sick. I'm kind of winging it here." She glanced at Slater. "Is this your husband?"

Marion laughed. "We're not together."

"If it's a delivery," Paola said, eyeing Slater, "you can leave it behind the desk. I can sign for it if you're quick."

"I'm not the help," Slater snapped. "I need to see the doctor. I'm thinking that's you."

"I'm not going to be able to do much for

you. I'm a gynecologist." Her expression shifted. "Wait—are you trans?"

"It's not a medical issue. I'm an insurance investigator. I'm here about an incident concerning a statue."

Paola's face clouded. "Fine, but you'll have to wait. Marion has an appointment." To the woman, she said, "Come on back," but then hesitated, eyeing the little girl on the floor with her book.

Slater knew what she was thinking—no way did she want to leave the kid alone with a stranger, especially one who looked like a delivery driver. He walked a few paces away from the counter and dropped into a chair.

Paola called to the guy on the other side of the room. "Zane, isn't it? Can you keep an eye on Ashley?"

The guy looked up at her, pushing his hair out of his eyes. "Fine," he said flatly, then went back to his phone.

Paola and Marion walked into the back, and Slater eyed Zane. He was good-looking, but young, with a fringe of blond hair that fell over his ears. His legs showed athletic musculature, and Slater had definitely noticed his butt on the way in. Sensing Slater's gaze, he glanced up warily.

"How old are you?" Slater said.

"Sixteen … why?"

"No reason."

Over by the counter, the girl on the floor called to him, "I'm eight."

"Really?" Slater said, eyeing her dubiously. "You don't look a day over seven."

"It's true," she said. "I'm eight."

"Can I see some ID?"

Zane chuckled, watching them interact.

"I don't have ID," she said flatly.

"So what do you do for a living?"

"I don't have a job," she said, as if he were a bit simple. "I'm a child."

"What's the pay like for that?"

"I don't get paid," she said, and laughed. "Come and look at my magic castle book."

"Can you hold it up to show me?"

"You have to come down here. It's all set up already."

Slater sighed and went over, dropping to the floor and sitting cross-legged, facing her across the book.

"Your mom is Dr. Paola?" Slater said.

"Correct."

"It's a weekday. Why aren't you in school?"

"It's a holiday," she said, flipping pages in the book. "Usually Cheryl is here when it's a holiday."

"Cheryl is the receptionist?"

"Correct. She's the boss."

"Not Dr. Paola?"

"Mom works in the back," she said. "Cheryl

sits here and tells everyone what to do. Although maybe Li is the real boss. He's the one who yells at mom."

"That sounds serious."

"You're supposed to be looking at the book," she said, frowning at him.

"You're supposed to be explaining it to me," he said.

"So this is the castle," she said, pointing it out, and then flipped the page.

Slater leaned back on his hands to listen.

A while later, when Marion came out of the back, Slater was still on the floor.

She stopped to take in the scene, then laughed. "How did you get glitter on your cheeks?"

"Ashley here has a big old roll-on pen loaded with it," Slater said.

"It takes a self-confident man to wear a tiara."

He reached up to pull it out of his hair. "Unfortunately it's a little small for me."

Zane got up and said impatiently, "Mom— let's go."

Marion walked over to join him, and they went out into the daylight. Paola stepped out of the back.

"What's this?" she said.

"I'm the pretty princess," Slater said, looking up at her.

"We both are," Ashley said.

"You're a good sport," Paola said, "but once you get that glitter on you, you'll be finding it everywhere for months."

Slater got to his feet and handed the tiara to Ashley. "I guess that's the price of being a princess."

"Slater says beauty is painful, but it's worth it," Ashley said, looking up at them.

"Thanks for presenting that valuable life lesson," Paola said, her brow furrowing. "Come into my office."

"Is Ashley OK here on her own?"

"I'll hear the chime on the front door." To Ashley, she said, "Come to my office if you need me, sweetheart."

As he followed her into the back, Slater saw a door at the end of the hall marked as a fire exit—that had to be the way to the alley, the door that Jordan had come through. Paola went into the first office and waited for Slater to enter, then closed the door and stood behind her desk as he took the chair in front. There was no Asian art in here at all—just her framed college degrees and an ugly close-up of an orchid.

"Gummy bear?" Paola said, holding a jar of candy toward him.

Slater shook his head. "Those are never vegan."

Her eyebrows shot up. "You don't look like a vegan. Where are you from, exactly?"

"Los Angeles."

"Of course you are. That's so LA." She set the jar aside and sat down. "So who do you work for?"

"Cudahy Mutual Insurance." Slater dug a business card out of his pocket and reached across the desk to hand it to her.

After she studied it for a moment, she looked up at him. "Why is an insurance company concerned about the robbery? The statue wasn't insured."

"The man who took it from you that day jumped bail. That involved a lot of forfeited cash. Tell me about the robbery."

Paola reached behind her and pulled a tissue from a box, then rose briefly to hand it to him. "I can't take you seriously with the glitter on your face."

"It seems that Ashley has me on her sucker list," Slater said, and wiped his cheeks.

"I don't know what I can tell you. A man broke in the back door and waved a gun around."

"Did he break the lock, or was it open?"

"He had a crowbar."

"Can I see the damage?"

Paola shifted uncomfortably. "Technically he didn't break anything, but he managed to get in through a locked door."

"What did he take?"

"I don't have a cash drawer, so he took the artwork."

"Did he ask for the cash drawer?"

"I'd have to check with Cheryl, my receptionist. She talked to him first. I know that all he got away with was the statue."

"What does it look like?"

"About this tall," she said, holding her palm above her desk. "It's a Chinese princess, or a queen. The surface is gray and distressed."

"Did you get the statue back when they arrested the culprit?"

Her eyes grew wide. "I don't know what happened to it."

"Do you think Thiago has it?"

A flash of understanding flitted through her eyes, and she looked away, shifting in her chair and tucking her hair behind her ear. She was delaying, he knew, to give herself time to think.

"Quit stalling, sister," Slater demanded. "Tell me the truth."

"Originally I thought the piece had archeological value. Now I know it doesn't."

Interesting that Thiago had used that exact phrase, *archeological value.*

"So you're not going after Thiago?"

"Thiago can enjoy the fake. I don't want it."

"Did you tell the police that he was behind the robbery?"

"I don't know that he was. All I know is that a man came in here and took it at gunpoint. I had to pick him out of a photo lineup."

"You just implied that Thiago has it," Slater said.

"He might." She gestured nervously. "I don't really care. It's out of my hands anyway—the police were more concerned about the break-in and the gun."

"Where did the statue come from? Why did Thiago think it was his?"

"We bought it together at an auction in Los Angeles. It was part of a lot of several Asian antiques. We thought all of them were just decorative pieces, so Thiago took some, and I took others. Then he got the idea that the princess statue was worth something. He asked me to ship it to him. I suppose it's possible that he got impatient, and sent that fellow to retrieve it."

"Which auction house was it?" Slater said, watching her.

"You're an Angeleno—do you know those places on Sunset Boulevard? One of those. We went to several. I don't remember which one specifically."

He looked around her office. "I guess all those other antiques are at your house."

"This is a place of business," Paola said. "I don't keep anything valuable here."

Slater watched her for a moment. She was stumbling over her own lies. Either the pieces were valuable, or they weren't. "Did you have the statue appraised?"

"Just before the robbery. That's why I had it here in my office. I asked an expert to drop by. He said it was a worthless modern reproduction."

Slater sighed. None of those auction houses would have sold it to her without clearly disclosing that. "I'm surprised there are antique Asian art experts in Las Vegas."

"You'd be amazed at what people try to use as collateral at the casinos," she said. "There's plenty of demand for those skills."

"So who is Li?"

Alarm flashed in her eyes, but just for a moment. "I'm not sure I know who you mean."

"Yeah, you do. He was in here shouting at you."

"You mean Li, the medical tech?" She sat up and leaned on her desk. "He's a supplier. He handles some testing for me."

"So he doesn't work for you?"

"Li is a contractor. He comes by once or twice a month."

"Where's his office?"

"He's actually based in LA. His company is called Nguyen-something."

"Why was he shouting at you?"

"It was just a business dispute. A billing issue. It's all sorted out now."

"Do you often have problems with him?"

"Why would your company be concerned about that?"

Before he could reply, an electronic chime sounded, and Paola quickly stood up.

"I have patients," she said, and held her arm toward the door. "You'll have to go."

Slater walked out into the waiting room, closely followed by Paola. Ashley was still parked on the floor with her book and her princess gear. A woman stood at the counter, eyeing them expectantly, and greeted Paola by name.

"My receptionist is out today," Paola said.

As he headed toward the door, Ashley called after him, "Bye, Slater."

He turned to wave to her. "Stay real, kid."

Pulling out his phone, he called a ride-share, then checked the time of his return flight.

THIRTEEN

When he walked into the small aircraft terminal, the clerk greeted him, and he told her his name.

"I love the glitter," she said. "It really makes your eyes pop."

"Thanks," Slater said, and absently wiped at his cheek.

"You're the last passenger to arrive. Since everyone's here, we might try to get an earlier slot. You should board now."

The plane did depart a few minutes early, and seeing that dusty desert rat trap recede outside the little window was a huge relief. He sat back to think through his morning.

Paola had blatantly lied to him, her story shifting as he sat there. Most compelling was what she said about the origin of the statue—it was wildly different from Thiago's version. That meant the statue was significant. Thiago had lied about things, and so had Jordan, but of the three versions, Jordan's had the least rancid stench to it. If he was the only one telling the truth, it was messed up that he was the only one sitting in jail.

Back on the ground in El Monte, the air was noticeably more humid, and the Thunderbird was cloyingly warm inside from sitting in the sun, so he blasted the air-conditioning. On the freeway he drove past downtown, headed for Thiago's office. As he approached the ramp into the garage under the medical building, he found an open meter on the street, and pulled in.

"Hey, Arnold," Slater said, stepping into Thiago's waiting room.

The flash of recognition on Arnold's face quickly shifted to anger.

"If you lay one finger on me, I swear I'll call the cops."

"If you tell Thiago I'm here, I won't have to hurt you."

"He's with a patient."

"I can wait," Slater said, and stepped up to the edge of his desk. He folded his arms and glared at Arnold.

With a heavy sigh, Arnold rose and went into the back. A moment later Thiago came out of his office, wearing a suit jacket instead of his white clinician's coat.

"What are you doing here?" Thiago said.

"We need to talk."

He frowned but beckoned him in and closed the door. A black wheelie bag stood in front of his desk.

"Going somewhere?" Slater said.

"Sacramento. Meetings. It's just overnight."

"Are they trying to take your medical license away?"

"The state doesn't regulate doctors, you dick." He stepped closer, peering at Slater's face. "Why are you wearing glitter?"

"You like it?"

Thiago put his hands behind Slater's neck and leaned in, meeting his mouth. Slater went with it—the guy was good at this.

Eventually Thiago pulled back and pressed his cheek against Slater's. "Can I smoke you?" he said softly. "I have a few minutes before I have to leave."

"How can I say no to that?"

Picking up one of his guest chairs, Thiago carried it to the office door and set it under the handle.

"No lock," Thiago explained.

"If you really want to keep people out, you have to kick it in." Slater stepped over and took hold of the chair, then propped it at an angle and stomped on the seat, wedging it tightly under the door handle. "See?"

Thiago grabbed his shoulders and pushed him against the wall, then dropped to his knees and unbuckled Slater's belt, pulling open his fly and taking him into his mouth. Slater spread his feet and leaned back, then guided him with his fingers gently on his head. When he came, he grabbed his hair to make him stop.

As he stood up, red-faced and panting, Thiago cracked a smile and squeezed his shoulder. Slater met his warm mouth for a moment, then ran a hand through Thiago's hair to restore its natty style.

Slater buttoned his fly and buckled his belt. "We should do you."

"I don't want to mess up my clothes. The memory of that will keep me going for a while." He leaned in and kissed Slater's neck.

"You're a very sexual person," Slater said.

He pulled back and laughed. "And you're not?"

"Why don't you have a husband or something? Guys like you are always paired off, and exclusive."

"Guys like me?" Thiago said, raising his eyebrows.

"People who are dialed in to maintaining appearances."

"I'm not opposed to being in a relationship, but in my experience, no one can keep up with me."

That rang true, Slater decided, and put a hand on his neck, and looked him in the eye. "Who's Li?"

Thiago froze for a moment. "Uh …"

"Don't lie to me."

"I have no reason to." He turned away and stepped toward the door, where he tried to move the chair. It wouldn't budge until he heaved on it to release it from under the handle. "Li works at a supplier. I do some business with him." Setting the chair near the desk, he turned back to Slater. "Why are you asking about him?"

"His name came up. He's connected to Paola Martín's practice too."

"It's not surprising that Li works with Paola. We're in the same industry." Stepping over to his suitcase, he said casually, "So you've been talking to Paola?"

"What does Li look like?"

"I'd say he's a flashy little guy," Thiago said, gripping the handle of the wheelie bag. "Wears expensive suits, and drives a sports car."

"What does he do for you, exactly?"

"Li is a go-between with the labs that provide medical tests. Sometimes he sources specialized equipment."

"So he works for a medical company?"

"He is a medical company. It's called Nguyen Medical Supply. That's a Vietnamese name. N-G-U—"

"I know how to spell it," Slater snapped.

Thiago frowned. "What exactly is your company investigating, anyway? Li has nothing to do with Jordan. I thought you were finished with all that."

"I said I was done with Jordan, not the investigation."

"But he's going away no matter what you report to your superiors, right? He did what he did, and they nabbed him. The guy is trash. Maybe you just need to let it go."

"Is he trash because you think he has lower social status than you?" Slater demanded. "Or is it because he's gullible?"

Thiago threw up his hands. "Because he's going to prison."

"You'd be surprised who winds up in prison," Slater said, and walked out.

There was no sign of Arnold in the empty waiting room, and Slater went down to his car and drove toward the freeway. The traffic was still fluid, and half an hour later he pulled into the surface lot across from his building. He waved to the attendant as he crossed the street.

Upstairs, the lights were off, with no sign of

Max. Rey Pascual was still guarding the front office, bony and regal, his scythe at the ready. Slater briefly stuck his head into Max's space, just to make sure it was empty. Max was probably still working that window-shade case.

Sitting at his desk, he woke his computer and searched for Nguyen Medical Supply. It didn't have any presence online, and he couldn't find a street address. The county database showed that someone had taken out a business license in that name, so at least it actually did exist.

Andy might do better digging up details. People paid him to do stuff like this, although he didn't call himself a hacker, instead claiming that he did "deep research." In any case, he usually managed to achieve things that Slater couldn't. Slater pulled out his phone and dialed his number.

"What's up, mothefucker?" Andy said when he answered.

"Do you have some time to work for me today? I need to get a street address for a business." Slater recited the name, and told him what he'd found on his own.

"If you're in a rush, it's going to cost you."

"Then you should get to work."

Slater ended the call and reclined in his chair, swinging his boots up onto his desk. His eyes felt dry, and he rubbed them with his palms. Freaking Las Vegas. It always sucked the life out of him. He was tired from the flying too. Folding his arms, he closed his eyes. Just for a minute, he told himself.

His phone buzzing on the desktop made him start awake, and he sat up to grab it and peer at the screen. It was Andy.

"I got something for you," he said. "Nguyen Medical Supply has an address on Alvarado."

"That's in my neighborhood." Slater grabbed a pen and scribbled down the details. "Good work."

"I know—you owe me five hundred bucks."

"You little chiseler. That took you ten minutes."

"Closer to an hour, but it's not about … the time—it's about the skill set involved."

"Fine," Slater said flatly, and hung up on him, then pushed himself out of his chair.

He had a vague notion of where Li's address was. That stretch of Alvarado was a seedy low-end district that so far had managed to escape gentrification. It wasn't really a place to run a business—not a legit business, anyway. Killing the office lights, he locked up and went down to his car.

Driving up Alvarado, the jacaranda trees growing on the verge were still in bloom, a purple canopy made more striking by the golden late-afternoon light. There was no signage for Nguyen Medical Supply on the building, and he slowed down to rubberneck.

The number on the building was the one

Andy had found. It sat between an auto-body shop and a run-down apartment building. A heavy barred gate covered the front door, and there were no windows. The facade was worn and neglected, with a sagging overhang halfway up that implied it might have been a retail storefront in a long-ago incarnation. On the walls around the entrance were overlapping patches of paint in a dozen shades of yellowy-brown, from years of regularly painting over graffiti. The city leaned hard on property owners who didn't do that promptly, so someone was taking care of the basics, but otherwise the place looked abandoned.

Slater turned onto the side street at the next corner and parked the Thunderbird. There was an alley running behind the block, he saw, and he walked into it instead of back to Alvarado. Parked at the rear of the building, a few feet from the back door, was a metallic purple Lexus coupe, in the space between the apartment building's chain-link fence and the long dumpster for the auto-body shop.

Thiago said Li drove a sporty car, and that he was flashy—this had to be his ride. There were no signs back here either, except the perfunctory KEEP OUT. Li wasn't advertising his business, but if he was driving this car, he wasn't afraid to be noticed.

Pausing to survey the back wall of the building, he saw that there were no cameras, so he pulled out his phone and snapped a photo of the coupe's license plate. Stepping closer to the entrance, he saw why Li didn't need video surveillance—the door was made of heavy steel, and the lock was a high-tech Masamune. Those had titanium parts and oddly shaped keys that couldn't be copied. The lock was as close to unbreakable as they came. Obviously Slater wasn't going through this door without an invitation.

Turning on his heel, he walked back out of the alley to the Thunderbird and opened the trunk, pulling out the slim jim that he'd confiscated the other night in South Park. He tucked it into the back of his belt and covered it with his shirt, then went back to Li's car.

No one was in sight, and he pulled out the tool as he approached the coupe. Leaning close to the driver's side, he slid the thin metal strip down into the door along the window glass. But it struck a barrier, and no amount of finesse could get past it. Newer cars were built to be more resistant to tampering. He pulled out the tool and concealed it again, then went back to his car.

Climbing into the Thunderbird, he started the engine. His apartment was just a few minutes away, and he headed there, into his garage, and waited for the door to roll down. Just past the nose of the car was a tall storage cabinet. At a cursory glance it looked like an ordinary thin-walled metal box from an office-supply store, but that was intentional, so it could hide in plain sight. In reality it was a heavily armored safe, bolted into the floor, and had a sophisticated lock.

Inside was all the illicit gear that he acquired from Svetlana, his Russian supplier in Glendale. None of it was irreplaceable, but he kept it locked up because most of it was illegal, like the device he needed now—a vehicle tracker. Unlocking the cabinet, he took out one of the little boxes, about the size of a cell phone and twice as thick. The black housing was unmarked save for the magnetic ribs running along one side.

Climbing into the Thunderbird again, he drove back to Alvarado and parked on the side street. Before he got out, he grabbed a pair of black latex gloves from the box he kept on the floor in the backseat and snapped them on. As he walked into the alley, he wiped the device on his pant leg to remove any fingerprints, then slid on the recessed power switch.

Svetlana's ingenious technology used cell towers and Wi-Fi signals to calculate its position, so it didn't need a view of the sky. Not reliant on faint GPS signals from space, it also used a lot less power—its battery would keep it working for several days.

The purple coupe was still here. Slater glanced around to make sure he wasn't being observed, then crouched at the rear tire and reached up inside the wheel well. It took a few seconds to find a metal part for the tracker's magnets to adhere to, but when he felt it attach, he quickly rose and stepped away from the car.

With that done, he could approach Li. The heavy door didn't have a bell, and there was no point knocking on it. Even if he pounded on it with his fist, no one inside would hear it through that steel. Maybe there was a bell around front.

Before he went to check, he pulled out his phone and opened the tracking app. Svetlana's tech wasn't cheap, and he had to pay her a regular subscription fee for online access to the trackers, but it was reliable. "Built like a Soviet tank," she had explained. "Not pretty, but it gets the job done." The controls in the app were clunky and labeled in a mishmash of Cyrillic and broken English, which meant she probably had the software built by her contacts in Russia. But like she said, it didn't need to be pretty—it needed to work, and it always did.

The tracker was already online, and the app showed a map with a superimposed green circle to indicate its estimated location, averaging the known positions of nearby cell towers and Wi-Fi points culled from public databases. The green circle was right where it should be, right where he was standing, encompassing Li's building and the apartment building next door.

Slater tucked his phone away and was about to stride off when the back door to the building creaked open. The guy who came out was beefy, with a big red beard, wearing a brown suit and an open collar. Under his jacket was the telltale bulge of a sidearm. Max had looked like this when Slater first met him—the archetypal heavy.

Behind him came a guy in a shiny gray suit cut to flatter his slender frame, his black hair styled in a trendy pomp. That had to be Li. As he closed the door and stuck an odd-looking key into that high-end lock, the guard pointed a finger at Slater.

"You can't sleep back here."

"Do I look like I'm sleeping?"

"If you pitch your tent in this alley, I'll light the fucker on fire, and burn it to the ground whether you're inside it or not."

"I'm not homeless," Slater said. "I was driving through the alley a minute ago with my truck, and I bumped the rear end of this Lexus. Is it yours? I was going to leave you a note and my insurance card."

Li was glaring at him now. "You did what?"

The guard scowled and walked toward the rear end of the coupe, but Li hung back at the door to the building. Slater walked toward the car. As he'd hoped, the guard was thoroughly distracted in examining the vehicle, looking for damage. As Slater stepped up, he sucker-punched him from the side, a solid blow to the jaw. He didn't lose his footing, but his head spun, and he gave it a shake, and then reached into his jacket for his weapon. But Slater was faster, darting in with his other hand to snatch it from its holster before the guy had recovered from the blow.

Stepping back a few paces, Slater leveled the gun at the guard. It was heavy, a .40 or a .45.

"What's with all the firepower?" Slater said. "Are you filming a rap video after?"

"You son of a bitch," the guy growled, rubbing his jaw, murder in his eyes.

Li wasn't alarmed at all—instead he just looked weary. "Mike, you're so sloppy. What did I tell you about being sloppy?" He jutted his chin at Slater. "Why are you wearing gloves?"

"What kind of bunco are you running here?" Slater demanded. "High-security locks, and an armed gorilla?"

"You're wearing glitter," the guard said, straightening up. "You're no tough guy. You're not going to shoot me."

He gestured with the weapon. "Don't test me, Mike. You might not like the outcome."

Mike stepped toward him, breaking into a stupid grin. Slater wanted nothing more than to punch that look off his face, but he waited, and stood his ground. Mike's bulk was intimidating, but it meant that he moved slowly. When he reached the optimal distance, Slater lunged at him and landed a full-force gut punch, then used the heft of the handgun as a sap to punch him in the face. Mike spun sideways and groaned, then started to go down. Slater kicked him in the ribs.

"Why do you make me do this to you?" Slater shouted, and kicked him again, then pushed him over with the sole of his boot.

Breathing hard from the exertion, Slater stepped back and eyed Li, who had a thin smile on his face. The fact that he was so composed meant he'd seen a beatdown before, and probably much worse. That meant Slater had to be careful with him. He tucked the weapon into his belt in the small of his back and stepped toward Li, briefly showing his hands. The guy wasn't armed—a weapon would have been obvious under that tightly cut little suit.

"I told him he was too reliant on the heater," Li said. "Big guys are slow. He needs to get in better shape." He peered at Slater. "You really are wearing glitter."

"Tell me about Guanyin."

Li laughed, exposing a row of perfect white

teeth. "I wondered what your game was. Are you looking for it?"

"I'm asking you what's going on."

"I've handed it off to the sellers, so it's out of my control. But I'm sure the delay is only temporary. Delivery will be to Juárez, just like we agreed."

"Delivery of what?" Slater demanded.

Li's eyes narrowed. "I thought you represented the client."

"I don't know anybody in Juárez."

"Are you working for the scalpel jockeys?" He looked Slater up and down, and his lip curled into a sneer.

He had to be talking about Thiago and Paola, Slater realized. "What exactly are they up to?"

"You're not in it with them? So you're the hired muscle. Personally I wouldn't have taken the job without knowing what I was getting into. I guess that makes you as stupid as you look."

Slater stepped up and slapped him, then shoved him back against the steel door. It was risky, because a calm thug was sometimes calm because he was skilled in some brutal martial art, which meant Slater would be the one on the receiving end of a beatdown. But if the guy went around with a bodyguard, he reasoned, he probably wasn't capable of defending himself.

Slater slapped him again, and Li blocked his

other hand and pushed him away. He was strong enough, but it wasn't a martial arts move, and the motion was almost perfunctory. Slater let himself be pushed back. Li's glib expression was unchanged, but his eyes were bright. Slater knew that look. Glancing down at his crotch, he saw the telltale bulge in his pants.

"Do you get off on smacking people around?" Li said, and shrugged to adjust his suit jacket.

"It looks like you're into it," Slater said, and stepped closer. He positioned his boots outside Li's patent-leather shoes, then grasped his biceps, giving them a squeeze, assessing his musculature.

Li put both palms on Slater's chest, but he didn't push him away this time, instead groping his pecs through his shirt. Slater leaned into him, gradually applying the weight of his body. The guy was slight, and bony, and Slater could feel his wood. When his nose was just inches from his ear, Li turned and licked his cheek, slowly running his tongue upward. Slater shuddered involuntarily. It was kind of hot, and kind of creepy.

He pulled back and met Li's eye. "Tell me what you're doing. How are you involved?"

"That's never going to happen," Li said, gently pushing him farther away. "But I'll tell you what might happen. If you don't back off, I'm going to tie you up, and fuck you senseless, and then slit your throat."

Slater watched him for a moment, and tried to parse the look in his eye. Curiosity, maybe, but mostly malice. "I believe you'd try."

From behind he heard the sound of something scraping on the gravel. Slater stepped back a few paces and saw that Mike was stirring, on his knees now and eyeing him warily. Slater pulled the gun out of his belt and popped out the magazine, then pulled the slide to check the chamber, and ejected the round that was there.

"What's the idea, packing this thing with a round chambered?" Slater said, sliding the bullet into the pocket of his jeans and eyeing Mike. "You're going to hurt somebody."

Mike glared at him, and laboriously got to his feet, tugging on the lapels of his jacket, but didn't reply. Slater showed him the weapon in his palm, then tossed it into the body shop's dumpster, where it landed with a *clang*. Pocketing the magazine, he walked down the alley toward the street. Neither of them followed him. At the corner he dropped the magazine into a sewer grate, then peeled off his gloves and climbed into the Thunderbird.

On the short drive to his apartment, he watched the rearview for the flashy coupe, but there was no sign of it. Once he was in his garage, he killed the engine, absently watching in the mirror as the door rolled down, then sat there for a minute to think.

Thiago and Paola were civilians, but Li was a seasoned lowlife, maybe a gangster. That changed things. It was too risky to mess with Li, or dig into his business. He'd wasted that vehicle tracker. But the fact that Li was involved with those croakers meant there was more to uncover, and that statue of Guanyin was dead center. It was time to ramp things up.

Steeling himself with a deep breath, he climbed out of the car and went upstairs. In the icebox he found a jar of peanut butter, and opened it to eat a couple of spoonfuls. He'd forgotten to buy coffee again. There was bourbon in the cupboard, he knew, waiting patiently to envelop him in its warm loving embrace, but he couldn't do that when there was work to do.

Untying his boots, he stretched out on the sofa and set an alarm for a couple of hours. It would be fully dark by then. Next he shot Max a text:

Can I borrow your pickup for a few hours?

His response came soon after:

You know where it's parked.

FOURTEEN

Waking to his alarm, he gazed at the darkness outside the dusty window for a while before he remembered what he had to do.

After he changed into a clean shirt, he went down to the garage and opened his storage safe, then loaded the devices he'd need into an oversize toolbox, and put it in the trunk of his car. Svetlana had told him to use a plastic one, because a metal box would interfere with the radio waves.

Next he pulled on a pair of dark-blue coveralls that he used sometimes for gardening, and stuffed a pair of black latex gloves in the pockets. What else? He ran through his plan in his mind. The heavy wire strippers, he remembered, and a ball cap. There was a blue one with the interlocking LA logo on it hanging on his tool rack, and he grabbed it and the strippers before he climbed into the Thunderbird.

The apartment building where Max lived was downtown, on the back side of Bunker Hill, near the strip of museums and theaters and concert halls. Slater could never figure out why he lived there, in such a sterile upscale place. It was low-key, Max said, attracting people like judges and politicians who needed to be close to the Civic Center but who wanted to slink around unnoticed. That was worth something, Slater had to admit, and at least the place was near the freeways, and not far from their office.

As he pulled into the ramp to the underground garage, Slater reached over and opened the glove box, scrabbling for Max's garage-door opener. Once the gate rolled up for him, he drove in and parked beside Max's little green Courier, a classic mini pickup from the early 1970s. It had a few dents, and needed a paint job, but overall it was a gem. The bed was empty except for a step-ladder cable-locked to the frame.

He and Max kept keys to each other's cars. Thinking about how Max had described their relationship to Jordan, the guy really did trust him, Slater realized, climbing out and opening the trunk.

Once he'd thrown the ball cap on the passenger seat of the Courier, and set his toolbox on the floor, he started the engine and let it warm up. It revved high, with its Japanese timing, but it sounded perfectly tuned. Shifting into Reverse and easing up on the clutch, he backed up and drove out of the garage, then clicked on the headlights.

The traffic had thinned out after rush hour, and the drive to West Hollywood went fast. Slater double-clutched to shift gears, getting a feel for the transmission. The gate to Thiago's driveway was rolled closed, and the Land Rover wasn't parked there. If he was only in Sacramento overnight, he'd probably left his ride at the airport. Lights were on inside his house, but that didn't mean anything. Slater parked on the street out front and sat with the headlights off for a while, just to make sure.

Eventually he was satisfied that the place was empty, and dug in the pocket of his coveralls for the black latex gloves, wriggling his hands into them. Last night he hadn't seen any cameras, inside or out, but just in case he'd missed one, he pulled the ball cap low over his brow. They were usually installed overhead to be out of reach, so the brim of the cap would effectively obscure his face.

Starting the Courier's tinny little engine again, he pulled into the curb cut in front of

Thiago's gate. He pocketed the wire strippers and climbed out, scanning the street for nosy neighbors, and seeing no one, reached over the gate and felt for the control cable.

It wasn't encased in a housing, luckily, and he notched it into the wire strippers to cut it. Made of bundled strands of wire, it didn't break cleanly, but eventually he got through it, and the tension in the mechanism released with a metallic *snap*. As he'd hoped, that severed the link with the motor, and the gate easily rolled open when he shoved on it.

Climbing back into the little pickup, he started the engine, then lifted the toolbox from the floor and opened it long enough to switch on his signal jammer. The only indication that it was working was the brilliant blue lamp that came on, so bright that it made him wince. Svetlana had built it that way so that it wouldn't inadvertently be forgotten later. He had to work quickly now—the jammer would knock offline any wireless cameras and alarm components that Thiago might have, but at the same time he was messing up the neighbors' cell reception and Wi-Fi. It was extremely illegal, and people who couldn't get online were prone to freaking out, so he couldn't leave it running for long.

Dropping the Courier into gear, Slater pulled into the driveway, then killed the engine.

He pulled the ball cap lower over his brow and climbed out, eyeing the stupid Mexican feather grass lining the driveway. He should have brought a weed whacker too. Hustling along the side of the house with the toolbox, he found the point where the coax and phone wires descended from the pole. Right below the drop was the utility box, and he pried it open, then used the wire cutters to sever the phone line and the cable. That would disable the alarm and any cameras, if they were old-school and worked by wire. For both wires, he chose a point near the middle to make the cut, rather than at the edge, so it would be easy to repair—he didn't want to be a dick about it.

At the side door, he assessed the lock, relieved to see it was a standard hardware-store model. The one on the front door was too, he knew, but back here he could work out of view of the street. From the toolbox he took Svetlana's lock probe and plugged it into his cell phone. That launched the key-reading app, which displayed a black screen and the word "готов."

The first version of the app had required a cell signal to refer to Svetlana's servers, but when he'd explained the problem of using the key reader in conjunction with the signal jammer, she had rolled out an update, and now all the necessary software was built into it, and it functioned offline. As he worked, Slater grinned at the memory. It had only taken her a couple of months. She'd summoned him to her workshop in Glendale and proudly announced "product upgrades." If only the legit tech industry worked as hard at getting things right.

The other end of the probe wire was key-shaped, and he slid it into the lock, adjusting it slightly until the screen on his phone went green and displayed a number: 314. The heaviest thing he'd loaded into his toolbox was the thick binder with dozens of pages of master keys. Flipping through the heavy sheets, he found 314 and pulled it out of its little pouch, then tried it in the lock. It twisted freely, easily unlocking the deadbolt.

Folding the binder closed and packing up the toolbox, Slater took a deep breath and pulled open the door. The alarm immediately started beeping. This was the kitchen, he saw, but there was no alarm panel on the wall. He hustled through to the foyer and squatted to open his toolbox, pull-ing out another device, a black case attached to a bell-shaped metal hood—the EMP generator.

Computer chips were delicate, and at close range the electromagnetic pulse this device cre-ated would fry any and all unshielded electronics. The metal hood was a reflector, necessary to pro-tect anything not in its intended path—his phone in his pocket, nearby computers, TV sets. Aimed at the right spot, it could even disable a car.

He held the reflector over the alarm panel, then pressed the trigger. The device emitted a loud *snap*. The panel instantly went blank and stopped beeping.

There was usually a control box for the alarm somewhere nearby, and he soon found it, inside the foyer closet, when he pushed aside Thiago's winter jackets. The painted metal box had a telltale cellular antenna on top—he'd been wise to start with the signal jammer. The box was somewhat hardened to tampering, and it could be locked, but Thiago had left the little key right here, probably where the installer had left it, sitting in the lock. Slater pulled open the box and covered the electronics with the hood of the EMP generator, then pulled the trigger—*snap*.

Heaving a sigh of relief, he went to his toolbox and switched off the signal jammer, dousing the brilliant blue lamp. Less than five minutes of disrupting the neighbors, he estimated.

The lights were off in Thiago's office, but he didn't need them, as the ambient light from the foyer revealed his target: the statue of Guanyin. Pulling it off the shelf, it was surprisingly heavy. The surface looked like painted plaster, but it had to be made of stone.

He needed something to wrap it in, he realized, and set the statue where it had been and trotted up the stairs. Thiago had nice linens, he saw, pulling open a closet in the hallway. He took an expensive-looking sheet, soft and luxe even through his latex gloves, and descended the stairs, soon to have the statue rolled up in it.

Before he left, he had to make it look like a regular break-in. Things had to be layered in the right order, and that started with the glass. Looking under the drapes that hung between the bookshelves, he found a huge single-paned picture window facing the driveway. It would be a waste to break something that big, and it would take so much force that the noise would attract attention. A narrower set of curtains hung on the side wall. The window here was smaller, he saw, pulling the curtains open, and it contained multiple panes. Hinged to open outward, it also had an old-fashioned latch. Whoever had done the house renovation for Thiago had chosen not to replace this window, likely because it only had a view of the side fence a few feet away.

Slater went back upstairs to the linen closet and grabbed a pillowcase, then went out the kitchen door and walked around to the side window. With the fabric held over the glass, he jabbed with the wire strippers at the pane closest to the latch and smashed it in. He had to move fast now, in case someone had heard that.

Hustling back inside, he unfastened the

window latch, treading carefully around the broken glass on the floor, then pulled a few books off the shelves and tossed them on the carpet. Next he opened all the desk drawers and dumped the paper he found in one of them on the floor. Picking up the statue in its protective sheet, he went into the foyer and took his toolbox. In the kitchen he pulled open a couple of drawers. There was enough stuff on the floor already, he decided, and left them that way, open but not dumped, then stepped out the door and locked it with the master key.

In the driveway he loaded his toolbox and the statue onto the floor of the passenger's side of the Courier, then climbed in behind the wheel. Backing out into the street, he revved the engine, then headed for the boulevard. A glance at the rearview reaffirmed that he hadn't been observed, and he took a deep breath to dispel the rush of adrenaline. *Let's see what happens now.*

——◆——

Rather than pulling into the lot across from his building, he stopped at the curb in front and put on the flashers. It was getting late, and the resident sewing factories were dark and quiet. Guan-yin was too heavy to tuck under his arm, so he carried her in both hands.

The office was dark and empty, and Slater

flicked on the lights, eyeing Rey Pascual. That guy was a lightweight compared to this thing. He set it on the floor behind his desk and crouched in front of the safe. To make room for Guanyin and her upscale satin shroud, he had to pull out a shelf. It was a tight fit, but there was still room for the cash box and the stack of paperwork when he piled them in beside her. After he spun the dial to lock the safe, he dropped into his chair for a minute to catch his breath.

But not for long—Max's pickup was waiting at the curb. Pulling off the latex gloves, he dropped them in the trash, then took off his coveralls and balled them up under one arm before he headed downstairs. Driving back to Max's place, he rolled into the parking stall beside the Thunderbird, then moved his toolbox into the trunk.

Before he started the engine, he sat there for a minute, debating whether he should check the hookup app. He'd been with Thiago today, and despite Andy's insinuations, he wasn't a sex addict, so he should just go home and crash. But he was amped up from the evening's work. He needed to blow off some steam.

Different neighborhoods had different kinds of guys, and even though Max's place wasn't that far from his own apartment, the app reflected the polarized demographics. Downtown guys were either wealthy or homeless, as Skid Row made up a huge chunk of the neighborhood. One of the giveaways was when a listing said "your place only"—people usually lost their housing before they gave up their phones.

As he was swiping through the options, someone named Sizzle messaged him with a dick pick. Tapping on his profile, Slater saw there was a face pic too. Sizzle wore his hair in the same wild twisty curls as Jordan. That style must be in fashion right now. The guy was fuckable, he decided, although the face photo looked like one of the professional head shots that actors used. Still, his direct approach saved a lot of time. Slater wrote back:

Where you at?

Sizzle replied with a room number at the Baltimore Hotel, not far away. Slater started the engine and drove down the hill. Unwilling to pay the exorbitant hotel valet rates, he cruised around until he found a street space.

Striding into the grand lobby, Slater admired the coffered ceiling and the mahogany lining the hallway, preserved from when the place had been built, over a century ago. Stepping off the elevator upstairs, he followed the room numbers and had almost reached the one Sizzle had given him when he turned a corner to find a burly guy standing in front of a door. Dressed in a dark suit, he had his hands folded in front of his belt—this was a bodyguard.

"You're blocking the number," Slater said, craning to see around him.

"What room are you looking for?"

"Don't question me, you goddamn rent-a-punk."

Slater stepped beside him to knock on the door, but the guard held out his arm to block him.

"Beat it, grease ball."

Grabbing his wrist, Slater wrenched his arm and twisted it backward. The guy hadn't expected that, and yelped as he pulled away. Slater dick-punched him hard with his left. As he doubled over, Slater shoved him to the carpet, then quickly frisked the guy—armpits, midriff, belt, ankles—in case he was packing a weapon. He wasn't, and Slater rose to knock on the door.

The guy who opened it was wearing a tight white T-shirt and stretchy blue underpants, his head shaved bald. He seemed vaguely familiar, for some reason, but it wasn't the guy from the hookup app with the great hair.

"What's going on?" he demanded, looking down at the crumpled form of the guard, who rolled onto his side, his face contorted in pain.

"Wrong room," Slater said flatly, and turned to leave.

"Wait," he said. "It's me—I'm Sizzle. What

did you do to my bodyguard?"

"Nothing's broken. He'll be fine in a minute."

Sizzle had a drink in hand, something amber in a tumbler, and he swirled the ice cubes, watching the guard on the carpet. "It's strange to see someone that big in the fetal position."

"If you're going to stand here and watch him," Slater said, "I've got other places to be."

"Christ, man—chill out," Sizzle said, and beckoned him in. Before he closed the door, he spoke loudly to the guard: "Catch yourself, Kenny."

Typical of an old hotel, the room was small, and Slater stepped over by the bed.

"You don't look like your face pic on the app," Slater said. "Like, at all. It's a photo of someone else."

"I used a friend's head shot. I have to." He grinned. "You can see why."

"Actually, I can't."

"You know me. I'm a public figure."

"I guess you do look kind of familiar," Slater said.

Sizzle beamed. "I know you know me."

"I don't think so. Are you a pop musician?"

"Small screen. Think about it. You know who I am."

"I don't have a television."

"Who doesn't have a television?" Sizzle said,

and frowned at him. "Are you not from around here?"

Slater put his hands on his hips. "I'm from the ninety percent of this town that doesn't live inside your pretty entertainment bubble. I know you aren't from around here—your dialect sounds Caribbean."

"Good ear. I grew up in Bermuda."

"That means I've been an Angeleno longer than you have."

"You seem upset," he said, absently swirling the ice in his tumbler. "I hope you're not going to flatten me too."

"Only if you want me to."

Sizzle cackled at that, then turned to the door at the sound of a sharp knock. He pulled it open a few inches and spoke quietly. Slater went to the window and looked out over the square and the city beyond, then turned back when he heard Sizzle close the door.

"Kenny wants to call the cops."

"They're not going to arrest me for defending myself," Slater said flatly.

Sizzle waved dismissively. "I gave him a couple of Benjamins and told him to take a break. I don't really know the guy. My management company sent him."

"So what are you into, sex-wise?"

His expression became serious, and he dropped

his chin. "Have you ever been with a black man?" he said quietly.

Slater scoffed. "Dude—I'm not one of your aspiring-actor casting-couch twinkies. You need to fuck me, or let me fuck you, or I'm out."

"Such a hard-ass," he said, and chuckled.

"You like it that way, I'm thinking."

"Oh, yeah." Sizzle pulled his T-shirt off over his head, revealing television-worthy pecs and rippling abs. "I've had a couple of drinks tonight," he said, and stepped closer. "I'm a little worried about performance, and stamina."

"You don't have to perform for me." Slater put his hands on his shoulders, feeling the warmth of his skin.

"I'm thinking you should fuck me, seeing as you're so bossy."

"That, I can do," Slater said, and leaned in to meet his mouth.

Sizzle grabbed his butt and pulled him closer. Slater could feel his dick tightening in his jeans. Stepping back, Sizzle pulled off his shorts and climbed onto the bed. Slater faced him and got undressed as Sizzle watched, his gaze intent. Climbing up with him, Slater explored his body, running his hands over his skin, amazed at how flawless it was. Leaning in, he kissed him again, exploring his mouth, and squeezed his cock.

A ribbon of condoms sat on the bedside table,

and Slater took one and rolled it on himself, then met Sizzle's mouth again and massaged his fingers inside him. Sizzle arched his back and gasped dramatically, flailing with one arm. Such an actor. Slater shifted closer, pushing up his thigh, and entered him, wrapping an arm around his waist, then built up the rhythm until he was pounding him. He had to focus intently to tune out Sizzle's loud groans, and vocalizations, and cries of "Yes!" Finally he came, straining into him. Afterward he flopped onto his back.

Despite his earlier concerns about performance, when Slater reached for him, Sizzle was rock-hard. With one hand around his muscular chest, Slater stroked him until he came, yowling and spasming wildly.

It was an award-worthy performance, but Slater didn't tell him that. Instead he stretched out and put an arm over his eyes. Beside him, Sizzle's breathing gradually slowed.

"I'm going to order room service," he said finally. "Do you want something?"

"I have to go," Slater said, and sat up.

He rose and pulled on his pants, then his shirt.

"Can I call you sometime?" Sizzle asked, watching him dress. "I'm in LA a lot."

Slater dropped to one knee to tie his boot and looked up at him. "Look for me on the app. I'm there all the time."

Before he stepped out the door, he paused for a moment and balled his fists in case Kenny was waiting for him, but when he poked his head out, he found the hallway empty.

Back in his apartment, he measured out his half-glass of bourbon, then killed the lights and stretched out on the sofa. Barely more than a taste, a dribble in the bottom of the glass, the paucity of it made him resentful. But he pushed that out of his mind, and set the tumbler on the carpet.

He wanted to check on Conrad, but he forced himself not to, gazing at the luminous sky outside the grimy window. It was late, and he knew he should go to bed. Instead he put on an episode of the *Sasquatch Search* podcast. Slater wasn't sure how he felt about the cryptic creature, but the narrator's calm voice carried him away from the metropolis, deep into the boreal forest, and he got lost in the quest.

FIFTEEN

His phone was ringing, he realized when he woke, and he scrabbled for it on the bedside table, and squinted at the screen. He didn't recognize the number, but that area code—702. Freaking Las Vegas. He picked up and answered groggily, "Ibáñez."

"It's Paola Martín," a familiar voice said. "Did you go after Li?"

"What makes you say that?"

"Li said some Mexican thug got up in his grill and roughed him up. That has to be you."

Slater rubbed sleep out of his eyes. "I'm not a thug, and I'm not Mexican. My father's people were from El Salvador and Honduras."

"Li thinks I sent you."

"Why would he think that?"

She was silent a moment before she spoke. "He's trying to get the statue back."

"Get it back? That means it's his?" When she didn't reply, Slater raised his voice. "Speak up, Doc."

"Li made it, or had it made, and I bought it from him."

"So it's no antique. Why does he want it back?"

"You don't get it," she said, her voice rising. "You don't know what you've waded into."

"So enlighten me."

"I need to keep Li off my back. Tell him you're not working for me."

"Only if you tell me why he wants the statue, and how you and Thiago are involved."

"I don't know anything," she cried, the volume of her voice distorted in the tiny speaker. "Stay away from me, and keep Li away from me."

"I don't really plan to be hanging out with that guy," Slater said, but she'd already hung up.

If any of that were true, and Li had made the statue, it narrowed the possibilities. Where low-lifes were involved, what flowed north across the border was drugs, and southbound was cash and weaponry. Li had mentioned Juárez, so maybe the statue was a vector for the profits of the drug trade. But why were those two sawbones involved?

Climbing out of bed, he went to look in the

cupboard, but there was still no coffee, and nothing to eat. After he washed up, he got dressed, and opened the tracking app on his phone. No way was he going to hassle Li, but if Li wanted the statue, it gave Slater bargaining power.

The estimated location of Li's obnoxious purple coupe was near his building on Alvarado, but it was moving, shifting south, the green circle growing and shrinking and hopping as it found new Wi-Fi stations and the software recalculated its position. Li was so close to Slater right now, and headed his way.

Slater trotted down to his garage and backed the Thunderbird into the alley. Watching Li's location on his phone, he saw it turn east on Wilshire. Slater headed that way, making a left and cruising with the sea of vehicles headed into downtown. In the traffic, the purple coupe wasn't visible, but he knew it was there—the map showed it just a few blocks ahead.

The circle stopped moving and went gray. That meant the tracker was out of the range of cell signals—probably in an underground parking garage. A minute later Slater drove past the point where the dot had stopped and saw that it was indeed a steep ramp leading down under an office building. And then he spotted Li—on the sidewalk, with that neatly coiffed pomp and another sharp suit, a purple necktie to match his wheels. His head held high, he strutted with exaggerated confidence.

Slater turned at the next corner and pulled in at a meter. Li wouldn't be walking very far. Climbing out of the Thunderbird, he hustled back to the street where he'd seen him, and caught sight of the shiny suit half a block away.

The streets downtown were crowded in the morning, a sea of people headed to their jobs, but somehow Li sensed that he was being tailed. When he stopped at the next corner with all the other pedestrians, waiting for the light, he turned back and looked right at him, meeting Slater's eye. Li shot him a withering smirk—a challenge.

Just as the light changed, Li dodged in front of the crowd, sprinting up the block. How had he spotted him? Slater wasn't even close. Jogging after him, he saw Li duck into the alley. Seconds later Slater turned in behind him. The narrow space was devoid of pedestrians, and there was no sign of Li. He stepped aside for an oncoming car and hustled up the lane. It was lined by the unadorned back sides of century-old office buildings, and he looked into the doorways and behind the dumpsters on both sides as he passed.

As he came up to a gap between two brick buildings, he saw Li pushing his way in through a heavy barred gate. Slater sprinted toward it, but before he could get to him, Li casually closed the gate, and twisted a key in the lock, setting the deadbolt with a metallic *clunk*. The bars went up several feet and ended in messy coils of concertina wire. There was no way to get to him. Li stood there to watch Slater through the bars.

"I just want to talk," Slater said, panting from the run.

He laughed. "I don't work with the penny-ante goons."

It was infuriating, how aloof this guy was. Slater pounded on the bars with his fists, then grabbed two of them and heaved, but they weren't about to budge. Glaring at Li, he let out a guttural roar, bellowing until his lungs were empty.

"Damn, *vato*—you make me chubby," Li said, and casually looked him up and down before he turned to walk toward the building's fire door.

There was sweat on his brow, Slater saw, and he was breathing hard. That was mollifying—the guy hadn't completely outsmarted him. At least Slater had made him run.

"Why Guanyin?" Slater called to him.

Li turned back. "Because people are superstitious. Nobody is going to mess with a religious icon."

Rattling his keys again, he twisted one of them in the lock on the fire door and disappeared inside.

Slater could run around to the front of the

building easily enough, but Li would either be gone already, or doing stuff in one of the dozens of offices—it was pointless. He turned on his heel and headed back toward the street.

In his pants his phone rang, and he pulled it out to check. It was Grace, his elderly next-door neighbor. Slater didn't really have time for her right now, but then again, she never called him. He picked up.

"Are you nearby?" she said. "Your front door has been jimmied."

"Damn it," he snapped. "Did you see who it was?"

"I just noticed when I came home a minute ago. I opened your door and called 'Hello' in my best fragile-old-lady voice, but there was no answer, no noise—I'm pretty sure whoever broke in is gone."

"I'll be there soon."

Hustling back to the street, he dodged the stream of pedestrians and climbed into the Thunderbird, then drove toward his apartment.

His garage hadn't been breached, he saw, watching the door roll up. As he pulled in, he eyed the tear-gas traps mounted above it, one at either side. They were still intact, their little green indicator lights demonstrating that they hadn't deployed. The armored cabinet was still closed, but before he went upstairs, Slater checked the handle to be sure. Securely bolted—no one had been in here.

Hustling up the stairs, he found his front door closed, but clearly damaged. Grace had noticed it because they'd used a heavy tool on the dead-bolt and splintered the wood of the jamb. Inside, the apartment had been tossed. He didn't have a lot of stuff to throw around, so it didn't look that much worse than it usually did, but someone had definitely been searching for something.

Slater stepped into the bathroom and sat on the floor in front of the sink, pulling open the cabinet doors, and reached up under the back of the basin. It was still there. He pulled out the dusty freezer bag and found his stash of cash, intact and untouched.

"Amateurs," he muttered, and opened the bag, riffling out two grand in C-notes, then zipped it closed and stuffed it back in place.

But they hadn't been looking for cash—they wanted the statue. He stood up and tucked the bills into his jeans. Luckily they didn't know about the garage, where the sensitive stuff was. If they had broken in there, they would have tripped an alarm that went directly to his phone, and they would have been drenched in military-grade Russian tear gas.

Paola's phone call had spurred him to leave his apartment. Maybe she was collaborating with

Li. Pulling out his phone, he checked the tracking app. Li's car was still downtown, still in the same spot. Slater had just seen him, so it wasn't Li who'd broken in here. Maybe his gorilla. But that seemed less likely than Thiago, or someone he'd manipulated into doing it, like he'd manipulated Jordan.

Stepping into the hall, he knocked on Grace's door. She pulled it open a moment later. In her eighties, Grace wore her hair in a gray cloud, and today there was concern in her rheumy eyes. In her youth she had been immersed in the world of lowlifes, and she helped Slater once in a while when he needed an operative to play the doddering elderly woman. It was all an act—Grace was sharp, and canny, and engaging.

"Did they get anything?" she asked.

"I don't think so. I don't keep anything in there worth getting."

"It wasn't random, I'm thinking—you were targeted?"

"Right. I'll tell you about it later. Are you going to be around today if I send a locksmith?"

"Sure thing, honey."

Slater dug in his pocket and gave her a sheaf of C-notes. "I might have my cleaner knock on your door to get the new key. Her name is Rosa."

"I'll be here."

"I owe you one, Grace."

"And I owe you many," she said, and smiled before she closed the door.

Back in his apartment, he found that the intruders had pulled everything out of the pantry, which meant there was a box of crackers, a bag of muesli, and three bottles of bourbon on the floor. Good thing he bought his booze in cheap plastic bottles—they were still intact. He'd forgotten about the muesli. How long had that been in there? Opening the bag, he gave it the smell test, then threw it in the trash.

The sofa cushions were across the room, but they weren't ripped open, so he tossed them back where they belonged, then went into the bedroom. The futon had been flipped over and lay haphazardly folded against the wall. It took a minute to pull it back into place. After he piled the sheets at the end of the bed, he texted Rosa:

> I'll pay you extra if you can clean up today. Get the
> new key from Grace next door.

Next he called his locksmith and explained the job, and told her about Grace. Calling the landlord wasn't even a consideration—it would take him days to do the work, and he'd use a cheap replacement lock. Slater's woman would do the job right.

He tucked his phone away and looked around the place. It wasn't that bad. After Rosa had been through, he wouldn't even remember that the place had been tossed. As he put some cash for her on the kitchen counter, his phone buzzed in his jeans. It was Thiago. Slater stepped over to the hazy window and looked down at the street before he picked up.

"How did you find my apartment?" Slater demanded.

"What?"

"Did you get another indebted patient to do the dirty work?"

"I don't know what you're talking about."

"Yeah, you do."

"I've got my own problems," Thiago snapped. "I woke up this morning to a series of messages from my security company."

"Are you back from Sacramento?"

"I am now. Last night they sent their patrol to my house to check on me. The alarm went offline, and I wasn't answering my phone. I mute it when I'm sleeping. Turns out I got burgled."

"What's their response time like?"

"They sent the car when the alarm didn't reconnect after an hour. They found the gate broken, and one of the windows, but no one was inside. The electronics for the alarm are completely fried."

"Sounds like they're not very prompt. You should get a better alarm company."

"You robbed my house," Thiago shouted.

Slater sighed. He knew it had been a dick move, but it was the only way he'd been able to take charge of the situation. "I don't know what you're talking about."

"Listen to me," he said intently. "Don't cut into it, or break it open."

"What are you talking about?"

"I'm serious. It's a really bad idea. If you bring it back, I can pay you."

"Why would I believe anything you say?" Slater said. "You've done nothing but lie to me."

"Why did you take it? Did someone put you up to this? You don't know what you're dealing with. Just give it back."

"To you, or to Paola, or to Li?"

"Me, you moron," Thiago snapped.

Slater hung up on him, then dialed Doris.

"My beautiful son," she said when she picked up.

"You have a friend who makes tchotchkes out of plaster, don't you?"

"You're thinking of Beth. She's an artist. She makes ceramic art."

"Is she still working?"

"Beth has to work. She doesn't have a pension like I do. A while ago she actually sold her house and moved into her studio. That man of hers is no help—he's never had two dimes to rub together. He lives off CalFresh."

Slater sighed impatiently. "Can you give me her number?"

"Let me talk to her. I'll get her to call you."

"Better yet, set up a meeting. I need to see her today."

"Why the rush?"

"It's for a case," he said, and ended the call.

In the garage, he pulled his heavy canvas duffel bag from the wall rack, and one of his gardening shovels, and put them in the trunk of the Thunderbird before he backed into the alley. On the way to his office, he watched the rearview, but he didn't seem to have a tail.

Max's car was here, he saw, as he pulled into the parking lot across from his building. He took the duffel bag out of the trunk and headed across the street. The few day laborers waiting for jobs in the sewing factories ignored him as he strode into the lobby. On the way up, his phone buzzed with a text from Doris:

> Beth says she's available today. Her studio is at the Brewery.

A second message had her contact details and the studio number.

"I'm glad you're here," Slater said, stepping into Max's office.

"What's up?" Max leaned back in his chair, pushing his keyboard aside. He was wearing his dark-red suit, the necktie loose at his collar. That color was intimidating, and wearing it projected strength—useful for dealing with clients.

Slater dropped into the chair across from him. "Are you meeting your window-shade client?"

"Leslie. I'm wrapping things up with her today. Delivering the bad news, and a hefty bill."

Slater outlined what had happened in his own digging—talking to Paola, and Li, and the break-in. "So I'm not sure if I'm being tailed. Can we switch cars for a while?"

"No problem—I love driving your old boat."

"Classic," Slater said. "Not old. Also, can I borrow your truck again for a couple of hours this afternoon?"

"I'm not going to be using it. Do you have the key on you?"

"Always. Sometimes I feel it getting warm in my pocket. I daydream about jacking that little beauty, and driving it to Mexico, and never coming back."

Max threw his head back to guffaw. "I don't know how far you'd get. At least it's cheaper to get it repaired down there."

In his own office, Slater squatted in front of the safe, twisting the dial to open it, and pulled out the statue. Why was it so damn heavy? It had to be connected to Thiago's insistence that he not break into it. After he put the shelf back in the safe, he rearranged its contents and locked it, giving the dial a spin to reset the tumblers.

Unwinding the statue from the sheet, he stepped into Max's office and set it upright on his desk. "This is what put Jordan in jail."

Max looked it over, then picked it up. "Christ, it's heavy. If it's bound for J-town, it's too small to have weapons inside it."

"It wouldn't hold enough cash to make it worthwhile either."

"You know what's heavy like that, and just as fungible as cash?"

"Yeah, the thought crossed my mind."

"I say we crack her open and see."

"Not yet," Slater said. "I've got stuff to do first."

He lifted the statue and took it back to his own desk before Max's gold fever got the better of him. Once he'd wrapped it in the sheet again, he tucked it into the duffel bag. Calling good-bye to Max, he carried the duffel across to the parking lot and put it in the trunk of the Challenger, then moved the shovel and his coveralls over from his own car. He glanced around the lot and the street before he climbed in. There were people around, pedestrians crossing the parking lot and a few waiting in cars, but no one seemed specifically interested in him. Maybe he was being paranoid.

The trip to the Brewery was smooth and quiet

in the Challenger, and he pulled into a parking stall next to a loading dock. The sprawling industrial space had been converted into dozens of little live-work studios for artists. Every time he'd been here, he got lost in the warren of multistory buildings and bridges and stairwells.

He passed a chunky guy wearing a dashiki who didn't give him a second glance, even though Slater was carrying the bulky duffel bag. Of course it didn't stand out in this context, he realized—artists needed tools and substantial materials that would resemble this cargo. He could walk around here with a chainsaw and no one would raise an eyebrow.

Not all the studios had numbers on the doors, and he followed a hallway into another building, thinking he should be getting closer. Pushing through a fire door, he found himself out on the sidewalk that fronted the boulevard.

"Fuck," he roared, the frustration making his heart pound.

After some further exploration, mostly by chance he came to Beth's studio, and knocked firmly on the door.

SIXTEEN

When she opened it and greeted him, Slater remembered her. Beth was older now, some gray streaking her brown hair. She had it tied back in a practical bundle, with a few stray wisps at her ears, and wore jeans and a dark-blue smock marked with earthy gray smudges. Clay, he realized.

The studio had high ceilings and concrete floors. If she was living here, the sleeping space and the shower must be in the back, through the curtain that hung across a doorway. This room was set up as a work space, with a big table in the middle and a potter's wheel under the window. The shelves along the wall were an array of tools and plaster objects and earthenware pieces, some glazed and finished and some raw, like gray terra-cotta.

"Well—you turned out nicely," Beth said, waving him in.

Slater stifled an acerbic retort. Right now he needed her help, and that meant he had to go through the motions of civility.

Beth closed the door behind him. "We were worried for a while there. When you were in your teens."

"About me?" Slater said, and frowned. "I only met you a handful of times."

"I used to hear all the details from Doris. You caused her a lot of grief."

Doris had dragged him to a parade of shrinks in his youth, and one of the techniques they had urged him to master, to make him more functional in the world, was to reflect people's expressions back to them. He tried to smile the way Beth was smiling as he spoke.

"Unfortunately, that's still an ongoing issue."

Beth chuckled. "So what can I help you with?"

Slater stepped over to the worktable and set the duffel bag on it. Pulling out the bundle, he unwound the sheet and set the statue upright.

"Can you copy this in plaster?"

"That's Kannon," Beth said.

"Someone else called it Guanyin."

She nodded. "Same deal, different country. She's called Kannon in Japan and Guanyin in China."

"Do you think it's old?"

"No way," she said, without hesitation, and stepped closer to look it over. "I wouldn't mistake it for an antique from a mile away. It's obviously recent."

"Would an art collector make that mistake?"

"I don't see how, unless they were strung out on acid."

"Why would someone think it was old?"

Beth examined the surface closely. "It's been painted to mimic the patina of age, so someone who knew nothing about antiques might make that assumption." She knocked on it tentatively with a knuckle, then grasped it in both hands briefly to lift it, and muttered, "Wow."

"Heavy, right? That can't be plaster."

"I think it's made of concrete. One of the new high-tech products."

"How can concrete be high-tech?"

"It's about strength and density. Most forms of technology evolve incrementally, right—airplanes look a little different than they did twenty years ago, and concrete is better today than it was twenty years ago."

"Can you make a copy of it? I need it fast."

"Sure. I can take a cast in silicone and reproduce it in plaster. I should be able to match the paint job. This thing is super heavy—I won't be able to do that."

"That part won't matter."

"Can I keep it overnight?"

"No way. It has to go with me."

Beth nodded. "Do you want to go grab lunch, then? It'll take me a little while."

"I really can't let it out of my sight."

"In that case, I'll enlist your help."

"What's this going to cost me?"

Beth pursed her lips and thought about it. "Four hundred?"

Slater nodded in assent and sat on one of the stools at the table to watch her work. Beth turned on the vent fan over her work space, filling the room with the sound of its whirring blades. After she donned a pair of heavy gloves, she poured a clear liquid out of an unmarked bottle into a little tray, then applied it to the statue, slapping it on with a paintbrush.

"This won't damage it," she said, raising her voice to be heard over the fan. "It's just a temporary coating so the silicone won't stick."

Stepping over to the shelves, she rummaged among the wooden components and pulled out a rectangular frame that was about the size of the statue.

"You're lucky," she said. "I have a mold box that will fit her."

Slater didn't ask what it was, and watched as she tightened the wing nuts at the corners and set it on the table, with the open side facing up. Next she pulled a plastic five-gallon bucket from the shelves and set it on the floor. From two big jugs she poured liquid into it and stirred it with a stick. One of the components was bright yellow, and the other was blue, and a minute of mixing turned them into a uniformly green goop. Beth poured some of it into the wooden frame on the table, then set the bucket on the floor again.

"Help me position her," she said, eyeing Slater.

They each took an end and lowered it into the green goop. Beth arranged little yellow balls around the statue on the surface of the liquid, and then waved Slater away and sprayed something from a pump bottle onto everything. Next she lifted the bucket again and poured the rest of the green stuff into the box, completely immersing the statue.

"That's going to be the mold?"

"Correct. It'll be dry in an hour. So we wait."

Pulling off her work gloves, Beth went through the curtain into the back of the studio, emerging a moment later with a couple of apples. She offered him one, and they both sat at the end of the table to eat them.

"Doris said you were an insurance investigator," she said, between bites. "Is this for a case?"

"It is, but I can't talk about it."

"I understand."

"You can't say anything about this to Doris either," he said, holding her gaze. "I'll make it worth your while."

Her brow furrowed. "I know how to keep a confidence, Slater. You don't have to bribe me."

He'd forgotten that she was from Doris's world—that rosy place outside the cesspool where people were basically good, and told the truth, and kept their word. When Beth finished her apple, she rose and ditched the core in the trash, then stepped around to the mold box and gingerly pressed a finger onto the surface of the green stuff.

"Weren't you dating a cop?" Beth said, when she sat down again.

"That's long over. He dumped me like a sack of hot garbage."

She frowned sympathetically. "If you were a woman, I'd say, 'Men are awful.'"

"Oh, I'm fully aware of that, sister."

"I know a couple of guys around here I could introduce you to. Art-world types, so they're broke, but they're decent."

"Don't do that," Slater said. "Don't expose your friends to me. I'm not good for people."

"That doesn't sound right. You've grown up— you're not a ruffian anymore."

He chuckled. "I'm still a ruffian, just older."

"Well, at least Doris managed to keep you out of a street gang. She worked hard to make sure you wouldn't get jumped in."

"Really?" Slater frowned, thinking about it. In a way it rang true. There had always been stuff for him to do after school—shrinks and sports and odd jobs.

"I know you're good to her," Beth said.

"I'm not so sure she'd agree with that."

"She told me that you were having an argument one time, and you shouted at her, 'What do you want from me?' and she threw up her hands and said, 'Roses.' Then you planted a bunch of rosebushes in her backyard."

"That was more of a squeaky-wheel type situation," Slater said. "I figured they'll be there for her once I'm gone."

Beth frowned. "Don't be planning to subvert the natural order of things. She'll need you to take care of her eventually, the way she took care of you."

Slater sighed. It was a dark thought.

"Think of what losing your father did to you both. How old were you when he died?"

"Thirteen."

"Nobody should have to go through that. I know it messed you up."

"Yeah, it was pretty bad," Slater said. "So who's your squeeze these days? Doris said he was some kind of deadbeat."

"That's a strong word," Beth said, and laughed.

"It's true that he's always broke." She talked about him for a while, and finally said, "Let's check the progress."

Standing over the green block in the wooden frame, she prodded it with a finger, then her palm. It had congealed into a solid mass. Unscrewing the wing nuts on the mold, she pried the walls of the box off the rubbery contents, then carefully lifted the top half of the silicone, peeling it off the statue.

"It looks good so far," she said, setting it on the table.

In the concave surface of the material was a perfect impression of half the statue, with bowl-shaped divots surrounding it where the little yellow balls had been. That would help line up the two halves later, he realized. Buried in the other half of the silicone, Guanyin bore no trace of green residue. Using her fingers, Beth gently pried the statue up.

"Hold the head," she instructed him, and then worked to release the base while Slater cradled it in his fingers.

Soon the statue was free of the mold, and Beth carefully looked over the silicone impressions, eventually straightening up and nodding in satisfaction.

"It worked perfectly," she said. "Next is the plaster. That takes longer to cure. Even if I pour it now, it won't be ready until morning."

"I'll come back then." Slater picked up the duffel and pulled out Thiago's luxy sheet.

"Can I photograph her before she leaves? It'll help me match the patina."

"Knock yourself out," he said, and watched as she snapped photos with her phone, rotating the statue to get images of all sides, and close-ups, even laying it down and photographing the underside of the base.

"She's all yours," Beth said finally, tucking her phone away. "It'll be easy to reproduce the paint job. It's fake patina, so I know exactly how it's done."

"Someone like you made this?"

"Not the concrete. That's not in my skill set. But I could have done the paint."

Slater wrapped the statue in the sheet and set it in the duffel bag.

"Do you want half the cash now?" he said, eyeing her.

She grinned. "I can wait until you pick up the reproduction tomorrow."

Outside in the daylight, it was easier to find Max's car than it had been to find the studio, and Slater was soon cruising down Main Street into downtown. He drove into the garage under Max's apartment building and pulled up beside the little green pickup.

No one was around, and he stood at the open trunk of the Challenger to pull on his dark-blue coveralls. Next he put his shovel in the bed of the pickup and lashed it in with a bungee cord, then set the duffel on the floor of the passenger's seat.

The station where idiot Conrad worked was a few minutes farther west. It didn't matter whether Conrad was there or not—what mattered was that Slater knew what the landscaping looked like, and that the yard next to a police station was one of the few public places where homeless people wouldn't be hanging around to interfere.

He pulled up at a parking meter along the open space adjacent to the building. Originally it had been a thirsty half-acre patch of lawn, with streets on two sides, but it wasn't golf-course green anymore, since the city had sensibly pulled out the turf and replaced it with drought-tolerant plantings and some walking paths. It looked great, partly because it was free of tents and sleeping bags and shopping carts, but mostly because whoever had planned it had chosen appropriate species.

What he was about to do might be a little suspicious, he realized, as it was late afternoon, a weird time to be gardening. Climbing out of the Courier, he grabbed the shovel and carried the duffel bag into the yard. There was a gardener here working with a branch trimmer, pruning back the incense cedar. This guy had to be on city staff—contract gardeners would have finished hours ago.

Slater set the duffel on the ground and approached the guy, lifting his shovel onto his shoulder.

"You're working late."

The guy paused for a moment and looked him over, eyeing the shovel. "Nine to six, like everybody else."

"Did you talk to the arborist?" Slater said.

"The who, now?"

"The tree doctor. She inspected your *Calocedrus* and *Fraxinus,* and hired me to aerate the roots on that velvet ash." He nodded to the duffel bag. "I brought my gear."

"I never heard anything about it," he said, and wiped his brow with the back of his gloved hand.

"It won't take me long. I'll stay out of your way."

"You won't be in my way. I'm not going anywhere near the ash." He turned back to the cedar.

"The palo verdes look great," Slater said, gesturing to them. "They're thriving."

"They love the soil here," he said, not looking at him, still working the trimmer. "Sometimes they don't like the inner-city air, but these ones seem to be fine with it."

"You've got some brown bark higher up. You need to prune those off."

He turned to meet Slater's eye, his brow furrowing. "I'll get right on that."

He wouldn't, Slater knew, but it needed to be said. Heaving up the duffel bag, he went over to the velvet ash and positioned himself on the far side of it, out of the gardener's direct line of sight. With the shovel blade he scraped aside the surface layer of bark, then started digging a hole, far enough from the tree that he wouldn't disturb the roots, and just deep enough for his cargo. The soil was in good shape, and made for quick shovel work.

Kneeling beside the hole, he glanced around. The gardener was ignoring him, and no one else was nearby. He unzipped the duffel and lifted the statue, still wrapped in the sheet, into the hole. Rising again, he quickly shoveled dirt over it, then tamped it down, and scattered the excess at the base of the tree. After he replaced the bark, he assessed his work. No one would ever know something was hidden there.

Lifting the shovel to his shoulder, he carried the empty duffel back to the pickup. The guy trimming the cedar must have run out the clock, as he was nowhere in sight.

He started the engine and listened to its tinny rasp for a minute before he put it in gear and headed toward Max's apartment. Traffic was heavy late in the day, and it took a while to drive the short distance, but he liked the challenge of double-clutching when he shifted gears, treating the engine right and making it purr. Max was home, he saw, as the Thunderbird was parked beside the Challenger. Pulling into the next space, he killed the engine and climbed out. After he took off his coveralls and put them in the trunk, he moved his shovel over from the bed of the Courier.

When he climbed into his own car, the driver's seat was in an unfamiliar position, and he took a moment to reset it and adjust the mirrors. Before he started the engine, he phoned Andy.

"I have your money," Slater said. "I can swing by, unless that would interrupt you fucking that junkie with the cheap haircut."

"He's in recovery," Andy said, "and he's not here. You can come over if you bring me one of those doughnuts."

Slater drove the few congested blocks to Broadway and parked in the surface lot behind Andy's building. The vegan doughnut shop was just a few minutes' walk, and he went in and picked one out, then carried the little box back to Andy's loft.

When he opened the door, Andy was wearing his usual T-shirt and boxer shorts. Slater stepped inside and pulled out a sheaf of C-notes, riffling through to count out five of them. He creased them lengthwise and dropped them on the table with the doughnut box.

"You know what I like," Andy said, stepping over.

"It's cream-filled."

"Like you're going to be. I've got … wood for you already."

Slater chuckled. "I need to shower first. I've been doing manual labor."

Stepping closer, Andy put a hand on his shoulder to steady himself, then buried his nose in Slater's armpit. "No, you don't." He pulled away and sat at the table. "But doughnuts first."

Slater sat across from him and watched as he opened the box.

"You didn't get one for yourself," he said, and frowned.

"It's a lot of sugar."

Andy scoffed and bit into the doughnut. It was mesmerizing, watching him relish it, enjoying it so intently. Such a beautiful man.

When he was finished, Andy met his eye and demanded, "What?"

"You have a bit of cream on your lip," he said, and tapped the corner of his mouth.

"Oh, yeah?" Andy raised his eyebrows. "What are you going to … do about it?"

Slater slid out of the chair, onto one knee, and put an arm on his neck, then leaned in to kiss him. There was the fleeting taste of sweetness from the speck of food, and then Andy's beguiling mouth. Sliding his hand up Andy's thigh, he reached into his shorts and took hold of his cock, already rock-hard.

Andy groaned and pulled back, then got to his feet. Slater gently pulled his T-shirt off, then pushed his shorts down, and wrapped his arms around him, kissing his neck.

"Come on," Andy said, and moved to his bed, stretching out on his back, propped up on his elbows. Slater got undressed, dropping his clothes on the floor. He stepped closer to the bed and then climbed up, straddling Andy.

Slater leaned in and mouthed his earlobe, sending a shockwave through his body. Slowly he lowered his weight onto Andy's frame. He knew he liked the sensation, as long as he didn't press too hard, and they lay that way for a while, luxuriating in the heat and sweat and proximity. A bottle of lube sat on the bedside table, and Slater reached for it, and squeezed it onto himself.

Sliding his cock between Andy's thighs, he put his hands under Andy's shoulders, and mouthed his neck, breathing in his heady scent. Thrusting between Andy's taut legs, eventually he came, his body shuddering. He lifted himself off Andy, and rolled onto his side, then grabbed Andy's cock. Andy leaned into him as he massaged it, his nose in Slater's armpit again, then in his hair, and his ear, his breath loud and hot. Slater stroked him until he came, his whole body spasming.

Afterward, entwined together, Slater drifted into sleep, comfortable in the heat of Andy's skin. Sometime later, Andy got up and went into the bathroom. When he came back, Slater was sitting on the side of the bed, buttoning his shirt.

"I have to go," Slater said.

"No, you don't."

"I'm working first thing," he said, wrapping an arm around Andy's waist as he sat down.

Andy turned to him and met his mouth, and they spent a minute lost in it.

"I could probably go again," Andy said, touching his forehead to Slater's.

"You drive me crazy," Slater said softly, and moved to nuzzle his neck. "Why do you do this to me?"

Finally he stood up and stepped into his jeans, and pulled on his boots, and left before he had time to change his mind.

———◦———

At his apartment there was a shiny new lock on the door, and a blue floral-print envelope taped above it. Inside were two keys and a note:

Rosa has the third key.

Grace knew there was no risk in leaving them here, as there was nothing inside to steal. The apartment was clean, he saw, stepping in, or at least as clean as it could be. Things were back in order. Thank you, Rosa.

Measuring out his measly ration of bourbon, he slammed it, then checked the time. He needed to sleep.

SEVENTEEN

Rising to his alarm, Slater took a shower and got dressed, choosing a clean shirt from the array Rosa had left hanging in his closet. Down in the garage, he went to the wall rack to choose the tool that he'd need. The post maul was a little heavy, he decided, and harder to aim accurately. Instead he pulled down the yellow-handled sledgehammer, lighter but still hefty, and loaded it in the trunk of the Thunderbird.

The Brewery seemed busier this morning, and he took the empty duffel bag from his trunk after he parked. It was easier to find Beth's studio this time. She greeted him with a smile and waved him in.

On her worktable sat the statue of Guanyin.

Slater stepped over and examined it closely.

"It looks exactly the same," he said finally.

"I'm glad."

He picked it up to test the weight. It was much lighter, almost insubstantial. Setting it down again, he dug in the pocket of his jeans and pulled out his wad of cash. Counting out six C-notes, he handed them to her.

Beth frowned as she took the bills. "I said four."

"I know."

"Why the bonus?"

"Because it looks perfect, and you work fast."

"I'm not sure I should take this."

Slater waved impatiently. "Do you have something I can wrap it in? An old sheet?"

"For two hundred dollars, you can have a new one."

Beth went through the curtain into the back of the studio, and emerged a minute later with a white bedsheet in hand. Once he'd carefully wrapped the plaster statue, he loaded it into the duffel.

As he was leaving, Beth said, "Give my best to your mother."

Slater set the duffel on the front seat of the Thunderbird and drove to Beverly Hills. There was always more traffic on Friday, but when he pulled into the garage under Thiago's medical office, it looked quieter than it had earlier in the week. Medical folks must favor three-day weekends.

He retrieved the sledgehammer from the trunk and held it in one hand, gripping it just below the head and aiming the bright-yellow handle down along his leg so it wouldn't be so visible. With the duffel in the other hand, he went to the elevator. A woman with sallow skin and a glaringly obvious synthetic wig boarded the car with him. She glanced at the sledgehammer as they rode up, concern in her eyes.

"You in construction?" she said. "Is one of the doctors remodeling his office?"

"I'm the exterminator," Slater said, eyeing her sidelong. "I'm trying to catch a rat."

"Inside the walls?" she demanded.

The doors rolled open, and instead of answering her, Slater stepped out and walked toward Thiago's office.

Behind the reception desk, wearing his burgundy nurse's scrubs, Arnold looked up when Slater strode in, and his eyes grew wide.

"Don't start with me," Slater said, and jabbed a finger at him as he walked back to Thiago's office and threw open the door. There was no sign of him inside, so he went back to Arnold's desk and demanded, "Where is he?"

"With a patient," Arnold said, scowling. "In the exam room. What's with the hammer?"

"Go get him."

Arnold hesitated, that familiar look of fear and anger in his eyes, but then he rose and went down the hall. Thiago appeared a moment later, wearing a white clinician's coat, followed by Arnold. Thiago's face was contorted with fury, but it shifted when he caught sight of the duffel bag and the sledgehammer.

"Guess what I found?" Slater said flatly.

Thiago took a breath. "Come in," he said finally, and went to his office door.

"I'm calling the cops," Arnold said, hovering behind him in the hall.

"Don't do that," Thiago said sharply. "This doesn't concern you."

Slater stepped into his office, and Thiago closed the door behind them.

"What do you mean, you found it?" Thiago demanded. "You stole that from my house."

"If you want to sling a wild accusation like that, you should let your stooge out there call the cops. I'd be happy to explain to them about Li and Paola Martín."

Thiago glared at him but didn't budge. "Why are you carrying a demolition hammer?"

Slater went to his desk and laid the hammer across the blotter, then set down the duffel. He pulled out the swaddled statue, unwinding it from its sheet. Once it was exposed, he set it upright on the corner of the desk, manipulating it with both hands so that it would appear as heavy as the original.

"Tell me what's inside it," Slater said.

"It's just an old statue, Slater. I already told you—it came from an antique store."

"You also told me not to break it. It's heavy as fuck."

"Thank you for returning it," Thiago said, and gestured toward the door. "You should go now."

Slater gently set the statue on its side, then picked up the sledgehammer and hefted it over his shoulder. "I asked you a question."

His eyes grew wide, and he straightened up. "Don't even joke around about that."

Heaving the hammer high in the air, Slater swung it down, taking a step at the same time and striking the guest chair in front of Thiago's desk. The wooden parts splintered with an angry shriek, surprisingly easily, and it lay in a jumble of broken wood and fabric. It was exactly the dramatic effect he'd hoped for.

"You fucking psycho," Thiago shouted, his eyes wide.

Slater lifted the hammer again. "What's in it?"

Thiago pressed his mouth into a tight line and shook his head. Slater stepped back and aimed at the statue.

"Stop it," Thiago cried, waving his hands. "It's

radioactive, OK? If you break it, you'll poison everyone in the building."

Cocking his head, Slater stared at him for a moment. "I don't think I believe you." He lifted the hammer again.

"Stop," he shouted. "It's true. It's packed with cesium-137."

Slater rested the hammer on his shoulder. "Which is—what?"

"It's a metal. It's used in medical imaging and radiation treatment, but only in very small quantities. That there is a whole lot of it."

"How did it get inside the statue?"

"Li stole it somewhere in the supply chain. I don't know the details." He pushed a hand through his hair and took a breath. "He offered it to Paola to settle some debt. She thought it would be easy to sell it—the cesium was already shielded and hidden in the artwork."

"How are you involved?"

Thiago hesitated, shifting his weight from one foot to the other. Slater took the hammer in both hands again, and Thiago quickly held up a palm.

"I was helping her negotiate the sale."

"Who would buy radioactive cesium?"

"It's dangerous stuff—basically anyone who wants to cause mayhem."

"You sick fuck," Slater said. "You were trying to enable terrorists."

Thiago scowled. "You don't get to judge me."

"So why wasn't it sold? Why did you send Jordan to steal it?"

"We found a buyer, and things were progressing, but the buyer wanted it delivered across the border in Juárez. I knew that was a bad idea. Paola was going to do it anyway. The buyer was hounding her—and we had already accepted partial payment." He shook his head. "I knew she'd get caught and ruin us both. That's why I asked Jordan to take it from her."

"Why is Li still involved?" Slater said.

"He introduced us to the buyer, and the buyer started pressuring him. Li decided we were bumbling amateurs. He wanted to take it back, and sell it himself."

"So why was it sitting on a bookshelf in your house?"

"It's called hiding in plain sight." Thiago dropped his chin. "I wish you hadn't seen that. My libido got the best of me. I just couldn't say no to you."

Slater frowned. "I didn't invite myself into your house—you did. Why were you hiding it there?"

"I needed time to convince Paola to renegotiate the delivery. I told her it was missing, and that Jordan hadn't actually brought it, but that I was looking for it."

"I don't think she believed you, brother. But you're right that she would have taken you down with her—she's a terrible liar."

At that moment, the office door flew open, and Arnold burst in, brandishing a wooden baseball bat. It was an effective weapon to use in a surprise attack, but only if you landed the first blow—and Slater was too far from the door for that to happen. Arnold rushed at him anyway, waggling the bat like a middle schooler in PE class. It gave Slater time to dodge and swing the hammer low, aiming for Arnold's legs.

The handle connected with his shin with a sharp *crack*, and Arnold yelped in pain and tumbled forward. The baseball bat flew out of his hands and over Slater's head, landing on the carpet.

Arnold's face was a mask of pain as he rolled onto his back, wheezing and holding his shin. Slater reached down to grab the front of his shirt and punch him in the face.

"Why do you make me do this to you?" Slater shouted, and struck him again, snapping his head sideways. Blood trickled from his nose.

The guy looked dazed, and Slater forced himself to stop, forced himself to take a step back. Now there was blood on his knuckles.

"Idiot," he muttered, and leaned down to wipe it off on Arnold's shirt. Half-dazed and hurting,

Arnold didn't even flinch when Slater swiped the back of his hand across his pillowy belly.

Watching them, Thiago's eyes were wide, his mouth agape.

"Too much?" Slater demanded, eyeing him. "What did you expect would happen when you started selling stolen cesium?"

"You didn't have to hit him."

"You thought you'd escape the violence, I'm thinking," Slater said. "It was only supposed to happen to other people—when they got exposed to the radioactive crap you sold."

Arnold groaned and rolled onto his side.

"Spare me the high morals," Thiago said, recovering his composure. "You're a brute."

"I hit him with the handle, not the business end," Slater said, glancing at Arnold. "Nothing's broken. He'll have a little bruise on one of his shins. He's just being a baby right now."

Thiago's lip twisted into a sneer. "You're still a low-class brute."

"See, there's your problem," Slater said. "You're a snob. You said Jordan was trash too. That guy is a college graduate. He had a bright future ahead of him. You completely screwed up his life."

"Whatever he decided to do is on him."

"But you manipulated him into doing it. Other people don't exist just to satisfy your desires. No wonder nobody respects you."

"You," Thiago shouted, his face reddening. "You're the only one. I'm widely respected by my patients and my peers. By the people that matter."

"I don't think many people would respect a guy who tried to sell radioactive material to terrorists. That's way beyond sleazy."

"It's you," he snapped. "You're the one who's a fucking psycho."

Slater nodded. "I hear that a lot." He picked up the sledgehammer again and swung it high, aiming for the statue. As the steel head made contact, Thiago screamed "No!" With a resounding *crack,* Guanyin shattered into a thousand white shards and a cloud of dust. Thiago dropped to his knees, cowering behind his forearms. Slater scooped up his empty duffel bag and walked out.

EIGHTEEN

Once he'd ditched the hammer in the trunk, he pulled the Thunderbird out onto the street, punching the accelerator to dart across the southbound lanes in a break in the traffic. Merging into the northbound flow, he headed for Sunset Boulevard. With one eye on the road, he dug out his phone and checked on Conrad's location. He was at his station. Slater dialed his number.

"I'm at work," Conrad said when he picked up.

"Excellent news. Put your dick away, and zip up your fly, and wipe the drool off your chin. I've got something for you."

"Screw you, Slater. I'm busy."

"It's important. You're going to want to hear this."

Conrad let out a heavy sigh. "Text me when you get here."

The traffic was annoyingly sluggish, as it always was on the Westside. *You are the traffic,* Max had said. Whether that was insightful or not, it wasn't helping him get there any faster.

Slater wondered how long it would take Thiago to figure out he hadn't actually been irradiated. A cursory glance at the rubble on his desk would show that it was just plaster. He felt a twinge of guilt at how he'd treated Thiago, first sleeping with him and then breaking into his house. But the attraction had been merely physical for Thiago too, and he'd admitted he was deeply involved in a nasty criminal enterprise. Plus he'd treated Jordan like garbage—Thiago deserved far worse.

Beth's statue certainly hadn't lasted long. It had worked, though—Thiago had fessed up, had finally told him the truth. He understood Li's thinking now too, about the deference people felt for religious icons. It had felt a little weird to destroy the thing. But with her purpose fulfilled, and her existence over, maybe that representation of Guanyin had returned to the *bardo.*

Finally he got to Conrad's station, and pulled into a street space, then texted him:

Come outside.

Slater climbed out and stretched, then walked

over to the front entrance. A minute later Conrad pushed through the doors, frowning at the sight of him. He was in uniform today, all dark blue with the leather belt and that shiny silver shield on his chest. He waved Slater over to the accessibility ramp, out of earshot of people on foot coming and going from the building, and stood beside the globe mallows.

"What's going on?" Conrad said, resting his hands on his hips.

"I'd like to report a crime."

His brow furrowed. "One of the many that you've committed?"

"I just found out about a statue packed with stolen radioactive cesium. I know where it is."

He outlined the events of the last week, in broad strokes, starting with hauling Jordan to jail, and omitting the part about breaking into Thiago's house. Conrad pulled out his little notepad and asked him to spell Thiago's name, and Paola's. Slater looked at his phone to give him their phone numbers, and the plate number for Li's ugly coupe, and the address for his building on Alvarado.

When he'd heard it all, Conrad paused to rub his eyes before he spoke. "Where's the statue now?"

Slater pointed to the side yard. "Buried over there next to the velvet ash."

Conrad stared at him for a moment. "Come inside."

They walked through the service lobby and into an open room with a grid of desks, a few of them occupied, mostly by uniformed cops, but some in civilian garb. Farther back were individual offices, and Conrad stopped at one of them and knocked on the open door.

The lone occupant of the room was a woman, sitting behind the desk, her dark hair pulled back in a tight knot. She wasn't in uniform, instead wearing office drag—a white blouse and gray trousers.

"This is Slater," Conrad told her, and to Slater, "Sánchez knows about nukes and all that."

"The nontechnical term is radiological hazards," Sánchez said. She gestured for him to sit, then tilted her head toward Conrad. "Is this mook a friend of yours?"

Slater dropped into the chair in front of her desk. "Worse. He's my ex."

She cackled and eyed Conrad. "I guess you have a taste for *sabor latino*."

"He only looks Latino," Conrad said. "That's a story for another time." He eyed Slater. "Tell her about the cesium."

"That sounds like a story for right now," she said, sitting up. "What kind of cesium?"

"Cesium-137," Slater said. "Medical stuff."

He turned to look at Conrad. "Quit hovering. You're making me nervous."

Conrad sighed and moved to the side of the office, where he folded his arms and leaned against a cabinet. Sánchez listened intently as Slater told her about the statue.

When he was done talking, she said, "How did you get it from the doctor?"

"He invited me to his house," Slater said, gesturing vaguely and shifting in his chair, stalling for time while he tried to think fast. Why hadn't he thought to cook up a plausible story? "I saw it there, and I was under the impression that he'd stolen it, so I took it with me. I only found out later that it wasn't really an antique, and what was inside it."

"Why did you bury it here?"

He gestured helplessly. "This place was closed when I came by. I didn't want to take property that someone else had stolen into my apartment. I figured it would be safe to leave it overnight."

"It's a police station," Conrad said flatly. "It's never closed."

Slater eyed him. "My mistake. It must be the pace that some of you people do things. It makes it look like it's closed."

Conrad scoffed, and Sánchez cocked her head. "Still, you buried it. You just happened to have a shovel with you?"

"Slater is kind of a gardener," Conrad said.

Sánchez nodded and grinned at him. "It's not a bad idea to put it in the ground. Soil is an effective radiation barrier."

"I think it's already shielded," Slater said. "The quack had it sitting on a bookshelf in his house."

"I guess we'll see," Sánchez said. "Let's go dig it up." And to Conrad, "I'll get suited up and meet you out there."

Once they were in the hallway, Slater said, "She seems happy to have something relevant to do."

"Of course she is. It's the field she's trained in, and it's so rarely called for."

Conrad walked close behind him as they crossed the lobby toward the front entrance.

"Don't act like you're detaining me," Slater said sharply, eyeing him sidelong, "because you're not."

He chuckled. "You didn't mind a little of that back in the day."

"That was before you stomped on my head with your jackboots, and dumped my lifeless body in the gutter."

Conrad winced. "That never happened."

"It felt like it to me."

Slater led him over toward the velvet ash. A minute later a heavy olive-drab figure walked out of the gate from the parking lot at the back of the station. It was Sánchez, he knew, even though he couldn't really see her face. She looked like an astronaut. The suit was heavily padded, and she wore a hood with a respirator dangling at her neck, and carried a shovel in one hand and an electronic gadget in the other.

"Is that a radiation suit?" Slater asked as she approached.

"Yep," Sánchez said, and set down the gadget. "So where are we digging?"

Slater stepped over to the base of the ash and scuffed the bark aside with his boot. "Right here, about six inches down. Do you want me to run the shovel? You must be sweating already."

"Nope. Stand over there by the sidewalk." Sánchez pulled the respirator over her face.

A couple of other cops were outside now, Slater saw as he walked toward the street. They stood near the entrance to the station, observing Sánchez from a distance as she set to work with the shovel.

Conrad stood with him at the sidewalk, and they watched the painfully slow exhumation.

"She looks uncomfortable in that suit," Conrad said.

Slater pulled up a weed that had grown near the edge of the concrete, grasping it near its base to get the roots.

"Your gardener should have noticed these. This thing is ready to flower."

"They're full-time employees," Conrad said. "They're not paid for results." He watched as Slater plucked a leaf from the plant and chewed on it.

"Are you eating a weed?"

"It's a kind of mustard." Slater held it out for him. "Try it."

"I'm not sure I trust you."

"You trusted me enough to let me shove my dick down your throat," Slater said flatly. "Back in the day."

Conrad frowned but plucked a leaf and took a bite of it. "It tastes like arugula."

Across the yard, Sánchez set down the shovel and then dropped to her knees to lift a dirty bundle out of the earth. It took her a minute to unwind the sheet from the statue. Laying it on the ground, she reached for the device she'd brought.

"I'm assuming that's a Geiger counter," Slater said.

A minute later Sánchez pulled off her respirator and lowered her hood.

"It's just slightly above background," she called to them. "There's no danger."

As they walked toward her, Conrad asked, "There's no trace of radiation?"

"Not much, but there's definitely something there."

"I already told you," Slater said. "Cesium-137."

"There was a shipment of medical cesium that went missing in Las Vegas a month or two ago," Sánchez said. "It wasn't public knowledge, but I saw the alert. This is about the right size. I'd love it if it were all right here."

"That fits," Slater said. "The Vegas connection, I mean. Li works up there, and one of the croakers too."

The other cops had gathered around to see what the fuss was about. Sánchez waved one of them closer.

"Take this stuff inside," she said, stepping away from the hole in the ground, still cradling the statue. "I'll get on the blower and get this to the right people."

"You're welcome for me bringing it in," Slater said. "How much was the reward offered in your secret alert?"

"It wasn't secret, and I doubt anyone is going to pay you," she said. "You'll have to come inside and make a formal statement."

Sánchez walked toward the station, her gait awkward in the big heavy suit, accompanied by the other cops. Conrad stayed with Slater and folded his arms.

"Are you planning to hit them up for a reward?"

"Of course I am," Slater said. "Medical companies make more money than drug dealers. But first I have to find out who was stupid enough to lose that much cesium-137."

"I might be able to get a look at that bulletin she mentioned."

"The fact that they're trying to keep it quiet gives me a lot of bargaining power. I can tell them, 'Pay me now, or pay later with your stock price when it's on the front page of the *Daily Bugle*.'"

Conrad glanced toward the station. "If you want to come back later to make your statement, this might be a good time to slip away. If you go inside now, you'll be there for hours and hours and hours."

Slater nodded. That would give him time to polish his story. "You already know who to arrest."

"We'll start with interviews, but yeah, I've got the names."

"Then I'm done," he said, and strode toward the Thunderbird.

"Take care of yourself," Conrad called after him.

Slater turned back and flashed his palms. "I always do."

———•———

Also from Dagmar Miura

That First Heady Burn

The first book in the Slater Ibáñez series sees Slater running surveillance on an injured tech worker and tangling with blackmailers, party girls, late-night hookups with a gamut of guys, and a lot of bourbon.

slater.dagmarmiura.com

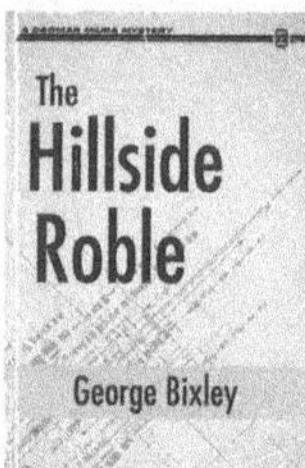

The Hillside Roble

Investigating a million-dollar heist at a gallery in the Arts District, Slater can't get a face-to-face with the owner, Eli, until he applies a little pressure. Eli turns out to be a minor celebrity, physically flawless but obsessed with his own image, and flaky in that uniquely LA way.

slater.dagmarmiura.com

The Mason Braithwaite Paranormal Mystery Series

No one is ever quite sure whether psychic investigator Mason gets results with actual psychic power or his more mundane flatfooting, but the disheveled redhead manages to resolve some intractable mysteries.

mason.dagmarmiura.com

Penstock Canyon

While helping out a friend suffering from late-night visitations, psychic investigator Mason is confronted with aliens on the roof and other liminal beings that have him questioning the very nature of reality.

mason.dagmarmiura.com

Truman and Celeste

Sometimes all a woman needs is a decent man—even if she's not sleeping with him. Join Truman and Celeste as they troll the gritty underbelly of Los Angeles, never hesitating to slam that cocktail, hit on guys, or ask the next relevant question.

truman.dagmarmiura.com

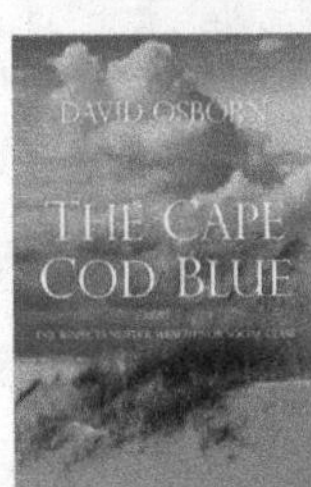

The Cape Cod Blue

The glittering, exalted world of art auctioning hides love, hate, and parricidal murder in a wealthy and socially prominent family when forgery of an anonymous Cape Cod painting is used to steal a world-famous portrait that's worth a fortune.

capecod.dagmarmiura.com

The Bone Bridge

Yarrott Benz, the 2016 Ippy Award winner for memoir, is forced to deal with extraordinary self-sacrifice in this harrowing account of teenage brothers, as different as night and day, trapped together in a dramatic medical dilemma.

bonebridge.dagmarmiura.com

The Psychic Vegan Cookbook

It has never been easier to cook vegan, and you don't even need to be psychic to do it. Whether your motivation is eating healthier or the welfare of other sentient creatures, Henrietta Flores guides you through plant-based versions of familiar dishes.

cookbook.dagmarmiura.com